PIGGY in the MIDDLE

Chapter One

Impatient as ever, Charlie pushed past his skinny sister Gina and left her to shut the front door.

'Mum!' he called, 'We're home!'

He chucked his anorak in the general direction of the coat rack. Gina managed to grab at it and save a pot of hyacinths from being knocked off the hall table. Score one to the ace netball player of Form 2B!

'I don't believe it!' Mum shouted suddenly from the kitchen. 'This report in the local paper,' she went on more quietly, 'It can't be true. It simply can't be.'

'Mum's always in a tizzy about some daft thing or another. What report is she talking about, d'you reckon?' Charlie asked Gina in a grumpy mutter.

'Maybe she's heard that the old Scout Hut is due to be pulled down?' Gina guessed. She'd overheard a boy at school complaining that the local Scouts would have nowhere to meet.

'No. That wouldn't bother Mum. She's not a Scout,' Charlie objected. Just lately he'd got into the habit of contradicting practically everything Gina said. Were all nine year old boys such pests, she wondered?

Pushing her floppy fringe of conker brown hair back out of her eyes, she hurried into the kitchen and asked, 'What's the problem, Mum?'

'This,' Mum said shakily, holding *The Upperleigh Gazette* up for them both to see. Because she'd been baking, there were floury fingermarks all over the front

5

page, and more down the front of her shapeless purple cardigan.

Gina read the main headline out loud.

'St Saviour's Hospital threatened with closure.'

'There you are,' gloated Charlie. 'I said you were wrong about the Scout Hut.'

Gina ignored him, because she could see how much the report had upset her mum.

'Perhaps the news isn't as bad as it sounds. The headline only says "threatened". There's no mention of a definite shut-down.'

'Even so,' Mum said sadly, 'I hate the idea that people may be thinking of wrecking that lovely old Tudor building, with the statue of Jesus over the door.'

The statue was a favourite of Gina's, too. It showed the Lord Jesus stretching out his hands to heal a sick boy. For as long as she could remember she'd loved the kind, understanding smile on the figure's face. She liked to think Jesus smiled at her in just that way, whenever she prayed to him.

'Practically everybody in Upperleigh has been treated at St Saviour's at one time or another,' Mum went on. 'You were born there, Gina. And you too Charlie, of course. Only it's Gina's birth I remember most clearly, because she was premature. Such a tiny scrap of a thing, that the nurses in the Intensive Care Unit insisted she looked like a skinned rabbit!'

She smiled at the memory.

'Those nurses were wonderfully kind to me, though,' she explained. 'They knew you were my first baby and that I was worried sick you might not pull through. Every hour, night and day, they went on checking to make sure your tiny heart kept beating.'

Charlie wrinkled his nose. For a moment, Gina thought he was making a face to show how bored he was with all the baby talk. But then he asked, 'Mum? What's that horrible pong?'

6

'Oh no – I forgot to turn the oven down!' gasped Mum. Gina made a dash for the oven, and took out a baking tray. On it were twelve black blobs which had once been scones.

Mum said, 'I was planning to serve them for your tea. Try scraping the burned bits off and smothering them with butter will you, Gina?' She took out a hankie to give her nose a good hard blow. 'I'm going to fight this hospital closure plan. I'd better start by ringing round, to find out how many of the people I know feel as strongly as I do.'

They watched her head for the front room, where the phone was.

'And meantime, we're to get our own grub? Charming,' grumbled Charlie. Actually he stood around doing nothing, while Gina had to hunt high and low for the butter dish. It wasn't on the pantry shelf where it should have been. Mum had put Tibby's milk bowl up there. She'd left the butter on the floor, next to his bowl of flavoured crunchies.

Charlie said that was typical. 'Once Mum's got some stupid good cause to think about, there's no room in her head for anything else.' Gina hated to hear him talk about their mum that way. She was two years older than he was and decided this was one of the times she ought to act like a real 'big sister' and try to talk some sense into him.

'Wanting our local hospital to stay open isn't stupid,' she argued. 'People need a place to go that's near where they live. Especially if they've been taken ill suddenly.'

But Charlie was too busy munching the first scone she'd buttered, to listen. He went out into the hall, leaving a trail of crumbs behind him. Gina found him there some while later, listening at the front room door.

'Mum's still on the phone,' he complained, 'Jabber, jabber, jabber!'

'So what?'

'Don't you remember *anything*? Dad's supposed to be ringing home tonight. If he tries to get in touch he won't get through. And I had something I specially wanted to tell him about my school project.'

Poor Charlie, Gina thought, as she watched her dark-haired, stocky brother stomp angrily up to his room. He really misses Dad. I do too, of course. The difference is that when Dad's not here, I don't get cross with Mum like he does.

She tried to share her worries with Jesus, in a prayer.

'Please Jesus, you know how I hate having to be piggy in the middle between Mum and Charlie. I think she could be right, and we ought to put up a fight to keep St Saviour's open. I don't want Charlie to accuse me of taking sides against him, though. Can you help me work out what I ought to do?'

Almost at once, she began to feel less panicky. What were the words of that lovely prayer everyone joined in at the end of each Sunday evening service? Something about the peace of God keeping hearts and minds? 'Thank you for giving me a bit of that peace, Jesus. It's wonderful to know that you're always ready to listen.'

Now she wasn't so hot and bothered, she remembered that Charlie's bad moods didn't usually last long. Anyway, it sounded as if he'd be too busy with his project to notice what Mum was up to. She smiled as an idea came to her, then popped her head around the front room door.

'Do you think Dad will be back at his digs yet, Mum? Only I know Charlie's waiting for a call from him.'

'Mmmh?' Mum was still sitting next to the phone, trying to make sense of the notes she'd scribbled on the backs of old shopping lists.

'Charlie's waiting to speak to Dad,' Gina reminded her again.

'Oh dear, have I been hogging the phone? Yes, I suppose I must have been. All right, I'll move into the kitchen to finish making this list.' She gathered up her notes and wandered off, leaving Gina to shout upstairs, 'Phone's free, Charlie!'

At last, Gina could get back to her job of scraping and buttering the scones. Luckily they didn't taste quite as bad as they looked.

'Here's one for you, Mum. And if that's the list of people who've agreed to help keep St Saviour's open, put my name on it, will you?'

Mum's eyes lit up. Through a mouthful of crumbs she agreed, 'I certainly will. Right at the very top!'

Next morning, nobody seemed to hear the alarm go off. The late start meant that Gina arrived in Form 2B with only a minute or two to spare. Her best friend, Tamsin Gerard, was annoyed.

'I was hoping you'd turn up early. I've got something terrific to tell you,' she claimed. 'You'll have to wait till Break to hear about it now though.'

'Can't you at least give me a hint?' Gina pleaded. Tamsin shook her head so hard that her hair swooshed around her face like red curtains blowing in the wind.

'There's no time,' she insisted.

So all through Assembly and the double period of maths that came next, Gina's thoughts kept wandering. Had Tamsin's parents finally given in and bought her the expensive new bike she'd been asking for? Or was there another reason for the 'I-know-something-you-don't-know' smile on her face?

The bell for Break finally rang.

'Race you to our bench, Gina,' Tamsin called. The two girls were both long legged, taller than any of the other girls in 2B. They reached their favourite seat in a dead heat. Not wanting to waste time arguing, Gina just grinned when Tamsin called 'I won!'

Eagerly, Tamsin tugged a brochure out of her pocket. 'What do you think of these chalets?' she asked, showing Gina a glossy picture of some A-shaped buildings, whose steep roofs sloped right down to the ground. Tall pine trees grew all around them, and beyond that Gina could see a lake.

'Where are they? Switzerland?' she guessed.

'Thought you'd say that,' Tamsin told her smugly. 'They do look foreign, don't they? Actually though, they're only seventy miles from here at a place called Green Acres. It's a sort of club. Members can hire sailing boats, learn to windsurf, or swim in a fantastic pool that's kept open all the year round.'

Gina was busy reading the small print under the pictures.

'It says here that membership is on a timeshare basis. What does that mean?' she asked.

Tamsin pretended to look surprised, and said, 'I thought *everybody* knew that.' She went on to explain, 'How it works is this. My father has paid in advance, so we can live in one of those chalets once a year, for the next twenty-five years. He says it's a real bargain, compared with the cash he'd have to spend renting a different villa in Spain each year. Of course, my mother will probably persuade him we need a Spanish holiday, too.'

Gina's mum had once told her that Mr and Mrs Gerard seemed to have more money than sense. Still, the Green Acres place did sound interesting.

'Anyway,' said Tamsin, 'our first timeshare week starts this Saturday. Would you like to come with us, just for the weekend?'

'To stay in your chalet, you mean? And maybe even learn to windsurf?' Gina asked excitedly.

'Of course. We could swim in that pool I told you about, too. Olympic size it is, with a wave machine and everything. You will ask your parents if they'll let you come, won't you? It'll be much more fun if the two of us go.'

'Mum's the one I'll have to check with. Dad's still in Sheffield, training staff for a new supermarket,' Gina explained.

'Great, she's bound to agree. She hardly ever nags at you and Charlie, does she? I always like coming round to your place, because she doesn't fuss if the place is in a muddle.'

Gina asked, 'How will I get back to Upperleigh if the rest of you are staying all week?'

'Oh, Dad's got to be here for an early morning meeting with his boss on Monday. He'll take you back on the Sunday evening.' Tamsin was turning the pages of the brochure. 'See these bunk beds we'll be sleeping in? Bags I top bunk!'

Gina got home later than Charlie that evening because she'd stayed on for netball practice. She found Charlie in the kitchen on his own, heating up a tin of spaghetti.

'It's not often you cook for yourself. Has Mum gone out?' she asked.

'No, but she might as well have done,' he sulked. 'Can't you hear the duplicator?'

Dad had kitted out their back room as his study, because he often had paperwork to catch up with at home.

Gina found Mum hard at work in there, feeding sheets of paper into the noisy machine.

'Can I switch that thing off for a minute? I want to talk to you!' she shouted. Once the duplicator had come to a chuntering halt, she began to explain about Tamsin's invitation.

'The chalet's in a marvellous place beside a lake – and the club members have all sorts of sports they can choose from – and Tamsin wants me to stay overnight on the Saturday –'

'Not so fast,' Mum interrupted. 'You're not talking about this coming Saturday, are you?'

'This coming Saturday, yes. That's OK, isn't it?'

Already, Mum was shaking her head.

'I'm sorry, Gina. You'll have to thank Tamsin, and say you'll be delighted to go with her some other time.'

Mum said 'no' so seldom, it didn't seem possible she could be saying it now.

'But why? You don't understand, Mum. The next timeshare week won't come round for a year.'

Surely once Mum did understand, she'd say 'yes'?

Charlie appeared, sniggering, in the doorway. He'd got spaghetti sauce all around his mouth. It made him look like a clown.

Using a horrible sing-song voice, he said,

'Mum's got a job for you to do, this Saturday.'

'What job? Mum – can't it wait?'

Still grinning his spaghetti sauce grin, Charlie snatched up one of the papers their mum had been duplicating.

'And I thought you *wanted* to save St Saviour's, Gina,' he said. 'Mum won't let you go with Tamsin on Saturday, because that's when you start helping her collect signatures for this petition.'

Chapter Two

'So that's why I won't be able to come to Green Acres,' Gina tried to explain next day.

'But if your mum wants you to help collect signatures, can't she take Charlie instead of you?'

'He's already promised to play hockey for the Junior school team. Mum reckons it's wrong to break a promise.'

Tamsin was totally baffled.

'Why didn't you pretend *we'd* made a promise, too? You could have told her we'd agreed to take part in a netball tournament, and that's why we were going away for the weekend.'

'I couldn't have lied. Not to my own mum!' Gina blurted out.

'I didn't say *lie*. I said *pretend*. There's a difference.'

'Not to me, there isn't,' Gina muttered. She'd listened to Tamsin 'pretending' plenty of times, as a way of wriggling out of trouble at school. And she'd always felt bad, even when it meant she escaped punishment too.

Perhaps now was the time for her to tell Tamsin 'It doesn't matter what name you call them. Lies are wrong. Jesus says so.' The trouble was, Tamsin and her parents never went to church. So Gina was scared she'd be laughed at, if she mentioned Jesus. And anyway, Tamsin had given up waiting for her answer.

'If you'd really wanted to come, you'd have found a way to fool your mum,' she insisted spitefully. 'Still, I don't care. There's plenty of other girls I can invite.'

Gina watched miserably, as she went across to speak to Brenda Tomlin. Brenda was a podgy girl, who seemed to catch more colds than anyone else in 2B. She also kept bringing notes from home, asking to be let off Games.

'Brenda,' Tamsin began extra loudly, 'I'm trying to find someone who'll come for the weekend with me, to a terrific place called Green Acres. I'll show you the brochure, if you like.'

'What for? Do you want me to say I'd love to come, just so's you can tell me I can't?' Gina heard Brenda ask suspiciously.

Tamsin draped her arm around the girl's shoulder.

'Of course not, Brenda. As soon as my mother suggested I could bring a friend along, I thought about you.'

She's 'pretending' again, Gina thought. And it *is* just as bad as lying, I know it is. Still, even though she knew Tamsin was in the wrong, it was hard to keep the hot blurry tears in her eyes from spilling out onto her face.

She didn't want to lose all she'd gained since she and Tamsin started going round together. They were good at the same sports, liked laughing at the same kind of jokes, were nervous of the same sarcastic teacher. But it was the differences between them that were even more important. With a confident Tamsin to back her, Gina had lost much of her little-brown-mouse shyness. Thanks to Gina's quiet warnings, Tamsin spent far less time in detention than she used to. We're a team, and a good one, she thought.

By lunchtime, everyone seemed to have noticed that Gina and Tamsin weren't talking to each other. There was a lot of whispering in corners, as various girls tried to work out why.

'Maybe Gina borrowed that posh party dress of Tamsin's, and spilled ice-cream down the front?'

'Or perhaps Gina caught Tamsin peeking in the history test?'

Gina wished she could explain exactly why Tamsin was cross with her. But they'd agree with Tamsin, that pretending wasn't the same as lying. She'd watched other girls being made fun of. It was horrible. She daren't risk being next on the list.

That evening, at home, Charlie started gloating.

'The TV weather man says it's going to rain on Saturday. It won't matter to me because I'll be in the sports pavilion playing video games, if our hockey match is cancelled. You and Mum are the ones who'll get soaked to the skin.'

Over breakfast on the Saturday morning he started again.

'Have you seen those grey clouds?'

'Shut up and eat your cornflakes,' Gina snapped. According to Tamsin, Mr Gerard planned to make an early start. So by now Tamsin and Brenda were probably giggling together in the back of his company car, well on the way to Green Acres.

'Time we were off, Gina!' Mum called. She was already in the hall, putting her brown PVC raincoat on.

'I wish you wouldn't tie the belt so tightly,' Gina grumbled. The style was wrong for anyone as tubby and short as Mum, making her look like a crusty cottage loaf.

She pulled angrily at the zip of her own anorak. The silly thing always jammed when she was in a hurry.

'Can't you leave it open? We don't want to miss the bus. I did tell you we'd be collecting signatures outside Sunglow Superstore, didn't I?' said Mum.

They headed for the bus stop at the run. Mum was carrying a plastic shopping bag, with a clipboard for the signatures.

'And I've brought along at least a dozen felt tip pens,' she explained. 'You'll have to make sure people don't

15

walk off with them after they've signed.' The job was beginning to sound horribly complicated.

'How am I supposed to do that? Yell "stop thief"?'

'No need to be silly, Gina,' Mum said sharply.

Their bus arrived in the town centre five minutes before the store was due to open. Mum bustled up to a group of housewives waiting outside.

'Have you heard about the proposal to shut down St Saviour's Hospital?' she asked them. 'You do realise what it will mean, don't you? Patients being sent to the City General instead. Relatives who want to visit them, having to spend simply ages on the round trip.'

'I hadn't thought of that,' one lady admitted.

'Then you'll sign our petition, asking the health authority to reconsider?'

'Sounds like a good idea.'

Before Gina could hand her a pen however, the town hall clock struck the half hour. The glass door of the supermarket slid open and the shoppers surged forward.

'Nobody's going to take any notice of us if we stand here, Mum,' she muttered, feeling an absolute fool.

Mum refused to be discouraged.

'We'd better change tactics,' she suggested brightly. 'Let's move over, next to those lines of shopping trolleys. They're jammed together so tightly people will have plenty of time to listen to what I've got to say, while they're pulling them apart.'

The rain was pelting down by this time.

'Lucky for us the trolleys are under cover,' Mum added, smiling at an old man with bristly white eyebrows, who walked like a soldier on parade.

'Now, sir – are you in favour of the scheme to shut down St Saviour's?'

'Certainly not,' he declared. 'Best little hospital bar none, St Saviour's is. I wouldn't be up and about doing my own shopping today, if the doctors there hadn't fitted me with my new hip joint.'

He printed his name, JAMES ELGIN, in big capital letters on the petition Gina held out, and encouraged her to keep up the good work. Before she could thank him, a man with a manager's badge on the lapel of his chocolate brown uniform hurried forward to speak to Mum.

'This forecourt is private property. You're causing an obstruction,' he told her. 'I'm afraid I'm going to have to ask you to move.'

'Sorry, I didn't realise we were in anyone's way,' Mum said politely. 'Come along, Gina.'

They moved out into the sleety downpour. Gina had hardly taken a couple of steps, before JAMES ELGIN's signature began to weep inky blue tears.

'Can't we sit in Carlucci's Coffee Shop till the rain stops?' she suggested. Mum shook her head.

'We can't give up now, before we've hardly begun. But Mr Carlucci may be able to help us, if I ask him nicely.'

She headed for the busy little café across the road, through a gap in the traffic. I can't remember the last time I felt so uncomfortable, Gina thought. Raindrops were dripping down from her anorak hood and hitting her nose. Cars were whooshing through puddles, sending beastly great sprays of muddy water over her legs.

In last Sunday's sermon, the vicar had said it wasn't worth doing things which you knew to be wrong. The knowledge that they were wrong, he'd argued, would make you feel bad.

'According to him,' she muttered to herself, 'I ought to be enjoying a warm inner glow, because when I agreed to help Mum, I did what I knew was right.'

And what was she doing instead? Sneezing, that was what.

'Atishooo!'

'Bless you,' Mum called, cheerfully.

Gina stared in amazement. Mum was coming out from Carlucci's trundling an enormous sun umbrella, its furled top a rainbow pattern of reds, yellows and greens. It had a heavy plastic base, which she was having to drag along after her.

'Wait. I'll come and help,' Gina volunteered.

'I persuaded Signor Carlucci to let me borrow it. None of his customers will want to eat outdoors in this weather,' Mum explained, once Gina had come to join her.

She rapped out orders in best sergeant major style, 'One – two – three – LIFT!'

'Everyone's staring at us,' Gina complained.

'The more the merrier,' Mum insisted. 'We need all the publicity we can get.'

They set the umbrella up close to the exit of Sunglow Superstore.

'The manager was only bothered because we were slowing his customers down on the way in. He won't care what they do once they've finished shopping,' Mum reasoned.

Sure enough, there were plenty of people willing to step out of the rain for a while on their way to the car park. The bright umbrella proved a marvellous gimmick.

'Without the umbrella of a local hospital, how will you manage?' Mum challenged passers by. Time and again she shouted. 'Make your opinion count! Sign our petition today!'

Gina had to keep replacing a page of signatures with a fresh, empty page because so many people appreciated the friendly treatment they'd received at St Saviour's.

'All my three kids were born there,' one shopper explained. 'I don't fancy trekking to the City General next time, where nobody knows me.' A teenage girl showed Gina the box of chocolates she'd just bought as a thank-you present for the nurses.

'They looked after Grandad so well when he went in for his operation,' she said.

At midday, the plump Italian who ran the Coffee Shop

turned up, carrying two lidded mugs.

'Minestrone soup for you, ladies?'

'Signor Carlucci, how kind. How much do we owe you?' Mum asked.

'Nothing. Is a gift. I also wish the hospital to remain open. Show me please – where do I sign?'

The soup he'd brought was tasty and piping hot.

'Remember how the vicar promised we'd get an inner glow if we did what Jesus wanted us to do?' Gina asked Mum with a grin. 'Well I think I'm getting one, now!'

Partly it was the soup which made her feel better. Partly though, she was pleased to be doing a job which everyone seemed to think was important. She was enjoying the chance to chat so easily with Mum, too. Somehow at home they never seemed to find time for a proper talk.

'What address do we send these signatures to?' she asked, some while later.

'My goodness, no-one will take much notice if we simply send them through the post,' Mum said, laughing. 'I plan to deliver them in person, to our local MP. I hope to persuade the Upperleigh Silver Band to lead the procession – we'll be marching on the Town Hall when he's holding a meeting there. We'll need banners too, of course. You and Charlie can help with the lettering.'

Banners? A marching band? Gina began to get butterflies in her stomach at the very thought. Charlie was sure to refuse to get involved. And what would Tamsin think?

'Mum?' she asked, 'you won't want me to march with you, will you?'

But Mum had stopped listening, and was trying to make out the writing on a sodden shopping list.

'C? A? Of course, I need cat-food for Tibby!' With only minutes to spare before the shops closed, she pelted for the Superstore.

'Wait, Mum,' Gina called after her. 'I think you told

Charlie you'd buy something *he* wanted, too.' Unfortunately, Mum was too far away to hear. And Charlie was bound to sulk. Gina could almost hear him accusing Mum, 'That rotten petition means more to you than I do!'

Chapter Three

'I thought my watch had stopped,' Gina said, as she wandered into the kitchen on Monday afternoon to check the clock. 'The time seems to be going so slowly.'

'You miss having Tamsin to spend your half term with; that's the trouble,' Mum told her. 'When did she say she'd be back?'

'Not till Saturday. Anyway, I'm not even sure she'll be speaking to me then.'

'Of course she will. She won't be able to resist telling you about the adventures she had at that timeshare place. But if you're at a loose end, you can help me collect stories about people who have special reason to be grateful to St Saviour's. The editor of the *Upperleigh Gazette* has agreed to find space in his paper for the most interesting ones.'

Gina started to panic. 'I can't go up to complete strangers and start interviewing them!'

'Of course you can't. I wouldn't want you to. Still, you're planning to go to the church youth club this evening, aren't you?'

'Mum, I only joined a few weeks ago! Most of the members are older than me, too. I'd feel awkward, barging in and asking questions.'

It was clear from the look on Mum's face that she couldn't understand why Gina should be so jittery.

'All I'm asking you to do is listen. Everyone likes to share favourite hospital stories. You saw that for yourself when we were collecting signatures for the petition.'

Gina began to chew at her knuckles. Couldn't Mum remember what it felt like to be the newcomer in a group of people who'd known one another for ages? Hadn't she ever stood on the outside, waiting for just one of them to turn and invite her to join in the chat?

By this time though, Mum's mind was on something else.

'Marker pens, for those banners. I must put in an order for them, before I forget –'

Because she felt so uncomfortable about what Mum had asked her to do, Gina dawdled on the way to the club. She stopped to look in shop windows at anything from houses for sale to fishing tackle. Even so, the hall was practically empty when she arrived. There were just two older boys – Graham Stott and Don Cullen – busy fixing up the table tennis table.

'Bring us the net, will you? It's in that box up on stage,' Graham called.

'Right.' Gina was pleased she'd been given a job. She handed him one end of the net, then took the other end to the opposite side of the table, fixing the net strings around their bracket.

'Fine. The tension's OK now,' he told her.

Here was her chance. She took a deep breath.

'Graham, I suppose you've never been a patient at St Saviour's, have you? Only my mum is getting up a petition to keep it open.'

'Good for her,' Graham said. He had one of those up and down voices, part growl and part squeak. Both he and Don wore their hair extra short, copying the hair-style of one of their favourite American Football players. 'Tell you who you want to see if you're interested in the local hospital, and that's my gran,' he added.

'Yeah, she goes there for physiotherapy, doesn't she? To help her arthritis,' Don remembered.

'Not only that,' Graham said with a grin, 'She knows

masses of stuff about the history of the place. Besides, there's nothing she likes better than a good long chat.'

He thought for a moment. 'I said I'd go round to do a bit of tidying in her garden tomorrow. You can come with me if you like.'

'Great!' said Gina.

During the evening she found several club members were worried about the scheme to close St Saviour's. One girl called Fenella talked about having her tonsils out there, ten years before.

'They gave me raspberry jelly to eat after the op. I've hated the taste of it ever since,' she said. 'Still, the nurses were wonderfully kind.'

Bart Ellis, the Youth Leader, had even more recent memories.

'My father would have lost his sight if he hadn't been given such marvellous treatment there,' he explained. 'Tell your mum, Gina – if she's looking for more volunteers, I'll be happy to do my bit. Upperleigh needs its own local hospital.'

On her way home, Gina noticed lights glowing behind the hospital curtains. They reminded her of how when she was born, the nurses had been constantly checking to make sure her heart went on beating. I expect there are more premature babies, in as much danger as I was, being looked after right now, she realised.

Glancing up at the smiling figure of Jesus above the door, she thought a prayer.

'Thank you for the skills you give to the doctors and nurses, Jesus. Bless those tiny babies and all the other sick people. Oh and please – don't let me get into such a panic about meeting Graham's gran that I don't listen properly to what she has to say.'

Next morning Mum was boiling eggs for breakfast.

'Yukk!' said Charlie, 'I'd rather make myself a peanut butter sandwich.' He went over to the pantry and took down the jar. 'There's only a scraping left. Weren't you going to buy a new jar on Saturday, Mum?'

'I suppose I could have put it under the sink with the cat-food,' Mum suggested. Then she remembered, 'My shopping list got wet. Cat-food was the only word I could read, so that's all I bought.'

'Then what am I supposed to do? Eat kitty chunks for breakfast?' Charlie snarled. Tibby spotted the tin mum had brought out. He started to curve his sleek black and white body around her ankles, to coax her into opening it.

'I'll pop round to the corner shop,' Gina offered, but Mum said no.

'Your brother's got two legs. He may not have used them to help us with the petition, but they're still in working order. Let *him* go.'

Gina picked up Tibby, and hid her face in his fur. She could feel a headache, like a narrow iron band, start to tighten around her forehead. I knew this would happen, she thought. I knew there'd be a shouting match. I should have tried harder to remember what was on that soggy shopping list.

Luckily, Graham called for her soon afterwards. He had a garden hoe slung over his shoulder.

'Gran's looking forward to meeting you, Gina,' he said. 'I was speaking to her on the phone last night, and she said she'd hate to have to go to the City General for her physiotherapy. If she has to travel by ambulance for any length of time, she gets very uncomfortable.'

The old lady was waiting for them in her sunlit front room. Her hair was creamy white and cut like a boy's, and so sparse that the parchment colour of the skin on her head showed through. She wasn't quite five foot high and looked as if a puff of wind might blow her over, the moment she went outdoors.

'I expect you're surprised at how little furniture I've got. I need to make room for my walking frame,' she explained. When Gina tried to imagine what it would be like, not being able to walk without pushing the clumsy metal frame forward one slow step at a time, she almost started to cry.

Noticing, Mrs Stott told her softly, 'There's no need to get upset. My hands and legs may not be as much use as they once were, but I'm given very good pills to stop them from hurting too much.'

Soon Graham had been told which flowerbeds to weed, and sent out into the garden. Perched on the windowsill, listening to the tale of how the local hospital had come to be built, Gina began to relax. It was such a fascinating story.

'St Saviour's was a thank offering, you know. Hal Whittinghame, Mayor of Upperleigh, had just the one son – a handsome, talented boy called Edward. One day in 1576 the boy was at his desk, learning Latin. A day later he lay on his bed, fighting for life. He'd been struck down by a terrible illness from which few ever recovered.'

'But Edward got better, did he? And that was what his father wanted to say thank-you to Jesus for?' Gina guessed. Graham's gran nodded.

'The doctor and nurse Hal called in used all their skills to care for him,' she went on. 'After a week and more when he couldn't recognise anyone, not even his loving father, Edward sat up and asked for his school-books. There and then, Hal Whittinghame promised to provide both money and land so that Upperleigh could have its own hospital, where other lives could be saved, as his son's had been.'

Gina knew what a splendid old building St Saviour's was.

'He must have needed a lot of land. And a lot of money,' she said. The old lady laughed.

'Luckily, he had both! His family had been millers in the town for hundreds of years. Also, because he'd decided to build a more modern wind powered mill, he was able to pull down his wooden watermill to make room for the hospital.'

She pointed to a brass log-box beside the fire. 'You'll find a picture of the original mill in there.' Gina lifted the box lid and took out a drawing showing a ramshackle wooden building.

'Oh yes – there's the water wheel. What's this lettering over the mill door?'

The words were really tiny.

'That we our Daily Bread may get,

Do Thou, Good Lord, this mill protect,' she read out loud.

'Hal's great grandfather is said to have composed that rhyming prayer,' Mrs Stott explained. 'There were no supermarkets all those hundreds of years ago. So bread was far more important than it is nowadays. In the winter many people had little else to eat, apart from salted meat and maybe a turnip or two.'

There was a regular 'chit, chit, chit' sound coming from the garden. Gina glanced out of the window. She could see Graham there, working with his hoe to dislodge a stubborn clump of weeds. Sensing he was being watched, he straightened to grin at her.

She waved, then realised she'd missed the next stage in his gran's tale.

'I'm sorry. What were you saying?'

'Just thinking out loud. Back in 1576, the folk of Upperleigh were lucky. The new windmill could grind more flour than the watermill, so they ended up with even more daily bread and a fine hospital as well.'

'We won't be so lucky if we lose St Saviour's,' Gina said. The old lady agreed with a sigh.

'I do hope the health authority can be persuaded to change its mind. I have so many happy memories of the old place.'

She started to talk about the first time she'd been a

patient there.

'Scarlet fever, that's what I had. And so did most of the girls I went to school with.'

'I've never heard of it,' Gina admitted.

'Think yourself lucky! Scientists found a cure soon afterwards. Several good friends of mine never came back to the classroom though, after the epidemic was over. Bessie, Evelyn, Rose . . . '

After a pause, she went on, 'Then my next spell at St Saviour's was when I was training to be a nurse. You'll never believe it to look at me now but I had a ward full of young airmen to look after in 1942. Terrible teases, they were. They used to call me Birdie.'

Gina smiled as she tried to imagine a much younger Mrs Stott in nurse's uniform, moving between beds like a bright eyed sparrow.

'And now I'm going back there to exercise these old hands of mine. The wheel has turned full circle. From patient to nurse, to patient again –'

In a moment or two Gina realised her hostess had fallen asleep. She left the room on tiptoe to join Graham in the garden. There was a smell of freshly turned earth, and a pile of weeds ready to be carried to the compost heap at the back of the bungalow.

'You don't think I've over-tired your gran, do you?' she asked as they shared this final job.

'If you have, she won't mind. She says she has too many hours to fill, and not enough to fill them with. And she hates that.'

'Then do you think she'd like me to come back in a week from now, to let her know how Mum and I are getting on with the petition?'

'Don't you dare *not* come,' Graham insisted.

Gina hurried home, eager to pass on all the information she'd been given. When she got back though, there was no-one in the house but Charlie. He was watching some daft cartoon on TV.

'Where's Mum, Charlie?'

'Wasting her time, collecting more signatures.'

'It's not wasting time,' Gina protested.

'That's what you think,' sneered Charlie. 'In our technology lessons this term, we're learning about inventions – and the teacher told us there's a surgeon at the City General who uses lasers to operate on people. St Saviour's docs wouldn't know how.'

Gina noticed that the characters in the TV cartoon were using laser swords to fight with.

'ZAPP! SPLATT! WHEEEE!'

'I reckon I'd be scared,' she said, 'if a surgeon used anything like that on me.'

'I wouldn't,' Charlie boasted. 'If I was ill, I'd want him to try all the up to date ways he knew to make me better.' He looked thoughtful and added, 'Dad's bound to agree when he gets home. He'll talk some sense into Mum. Make her see that she's wasting her time trying to keep the grotty old local hospital open.'

He picked up a huge half eaten sandwich he'd made, from the peanut butter Mum had told him to go and buy. 'Then she'll have time to do her own rotten shopping, won't she?' he growled.

Chapter Four

Early next Sunday morning, the doorbell rang.

'That'll be for me!' Mum called from the bathroom where she was washing her hair. For once though, it wasn't. Gina was surprised to find Tamsin on the doorstep. She'd caught the sun during her week at Green Acres, and her nose was peeling.

'We got back so late last night, I thought you'd be in bed if I tried to phone you,' she explained, 'but I've skipped breakfast this morning, so as not to waste any more time. I've got so much to tell you –'

Gina couldn't resist asking, 'Shouldn't it be Brenda you're telling?'

'Brenda! Don't even mention her name!' Tamsin made a face. 'She was only with us for two days, but it felt like two hundred years. Do you know, she refused to go near the lake? She was scared there'd be mosquitoes. At least, I think she said mosquitoes. Or maybe it was vampire bats?'

Gina laughed; she couldn't stop herself. She'd been half-planning to keep Tamsin at a distance till she managed to get an apology from her. But what was the point of spoiling the fun of being friends again, with a silly fit of the sulks?

'I know what you really came round early for,' she claimed with a grin. 'Your mother makes you eat muesli for breakfast. You wanted a share of our Sunday sausage fry-up. Come into the kitchen and grab a plate, before

Charlie wolfs the lot!'

The moment Charlie saw who'd turned up, he started asking questions. With his mouth full, of course.

'What was the windsurfing like, Tamsin? Did you get any lessons?'

'Yes, and I needed them. The sail took a lot of getting used to. I thought at first it'd be too heavy for me to lift.'

She mimed the way the instructor had taught her to reach down and catch hold of the control bar.

'Then he said I had to tug it up and lean backwards – like this. Sometimes I leaned too far though, and splashed back into the lake.'

'If I'd been there,' Charlie told her, 'I could have worked out the right time for you to stop going backwards.'

'Oh yes?' Tamsin said politely, not really believing him. But Gina nodded.

'Charlie's a proper wizard, when it comes to anything technical.'

She wasn't simply saying that to get back into her brother's good books after all their bickering about St Saviour's. Whenever Dad went away, Charlie became the family's Mister Fixit. Only the day before he'd shown Mum why her spin dryer wouldn't switch on. One of the wires inside the three point plug had worked free, and needed to be reconnected.

'Of course,' Tamsin grumbled, 'I'd be an expert by now, if I'd been able to take lessons all week. But my mother said "While Brenda is our guest, you ought to stick to the activities that interest her".'

'So what did she choose?' Gina wanted to know.

'*In*activities, mostly! She would insist on watching every single soap opera on the TV in our chalet. And she stared at all the post sports clothes in The Sun'n Shade Boutique, moaning because she couldn't afford to buy them.'

It was a relief to know Brenda had behaved so stupidly at Green Acres, that she wasn't likely to be invited again. Though really I ought to feel sorry for her, for not knowing how to enjoy herself, Gina was thinking, when Mum wandered into the kitchen with a towel wrapped round her head.

'Nice to see you, Tamsin. Do you want tomatoes with your sausages? And are you and Charlie having seconds, Gina?'

'I'm having thirds, if there's any to spare,' said Charlie.

We're back the way we used to be, Gina decided happily. Now so long as Mum doesn't mention St Saviour's — but it was too much to hope for. These days Mum's thoughts never strayed far from her fight to keep the hospital open.

'I wonder whether your mother would like to join our Save St Saviour's Committee?' she asked Tamsin.

'Don't suppose so,' Tamsin told her frankly. 'If anyone from our family is taken ill, Dad pays for us to go to the private hospital at Queen's Compton.'

'This private hospital — modern, is it?' Charlie asked eagerly.

'Yes, very. My mother went for a check-up at the Well Woman Clinic last month. They had all sorts of fantastic machines, to scan her brainwaves and everything.'

'Real sci-fi stuff, eh?' Charlie commented, fascinated.

'Oh well,' Mum sighed. 'Nobody can say I didn't try.'

Gina thought she looked really down in the dumps, and decided to ask her why, once Tamsin had gone. But Tamsin's tales — about steaming till she was lobster red in the sauna, and pigging herself on oozy cream cakes in the restaurant — put Mum's troubles right out of her mind.

It wasn't till Charlie had dashed round to his friend Jacko's house after tea, to help Jacko with a model aeroplane he was building, that she thought to ask, 'Who *has* joined your committee, Mum?'

'Practically no-one,' Mum said despondently. 'You've no idea how many people find excuses to back out, after promising to help. And I can't run the campaign like a one man band. There are too many expenses – for the posters I'm having printed, not to mention the cost of my costume –'

'Costume?' Gina repeated. Mum tried to change the subject.

'Will you be coming to the evening service with me?'

'Yes, of course. What costume?'

'It won't need to be anything elaborate. Perhaps if I asked the vicar, he'd let me use those old curtains from the organ loft?'

Mum seemed to be thinking out loud. She hardly said a word as they walked to church together. Then after the service was over, she went into the vestry to talk to the vicar and came out carrying a parcel wrapped up in old newspapers. I hope she's not expecting *me* to dress up, next time we go out collecting signatures, Gina thought.

Next day, when the girls from 2B were getting ready to play netball, she tried to interest Tamsin in Mum's mysterious mutterings about a costume.

'Once we got back from church, she took the parcel straight up to her room. I never got a chance to see what was in it.'

'Can't have been anything interesting, if she got it from the local God Botherer,' Tamsin said.

'The what?'

'My father calls anyone connected with religion a God Botherer,' Tamsin explained, shrugging. 'If he sees some bishop on TV, claiming prayer is the answer to the world's problems, he says that's daft. God probably stuffs cotton wool in his ears, the moment people start praying.'

Gina thought, Mr Gerard can't really mean that.

'What are you looking so shocked for?' Tamsin demanded. 'Go on, admit it. Church people don't know what they're talking about, half the time.'

'I suppose – some don't –' Gina muttered, uncomfortably.

'Of course they don't.' Now that Tamsin had cornered her into agreeing, she was her usual sunny self again. 'See this new pendant I'm wearing? You mustn't let Miss Warrender know because of the stupid rules about not wearing jewellery to school, but it's made from real silver –'

I've lost my chance, Gina thought. All I had to do was tell her our vicar talks plenty of sense – and so do lots of other people who believe in Jesus, like Bart. It's no good me singing 'Stand up, Stand up for Jesus' on Sunday, and then not daring to put in a good word for him the day after!

That evening she managed to have a word with Bart, before the Youth Club got into full swing.

'When you were still at school, did *you* have some Christian friends, and others who never went to church?'

'Yes, sure. Unless they go to a special church school, I should think practically everyone does, these days.' He looked interested. 'What's up? Come in for a spot of teasing about being a Christian, have you?'

'Not teasing, exactly. But there's a girl – and she's someone I really like, which makes it worse – who keeps wanting me to agree with her, and say things that are the opposite of what I really believe in.'

'Are you saying she does it on purpose?'

'That's the awful part – I'm not sure! She could just be repeating what she's heard her father say. Like today, when she told me he was sure God stuffed cotton wool in his ears, so as not to have to listen to our prayers.'

'And did you tell her what a daft idea that was?'

Staring down at the floor, Gina had to admit in a whisper, 'I couldn't –'

She was afraid Bart was going to lose patience with her. Instead he laughed, and said, 'I know! When I was your age, I had the same sort of trouble. I so much wanted to be liked by the real tough nuts in my class, I'd find myself pretending that the swear words they were using were funny – and then slink home, feeling like a worm.'

Bart was so good at running the club, it was impossible to think of him ever having had to slink around anywhere. She saw him wave to Fenella, who was coming in through the door with Don.

'Listen, there's no time to go into all this now, Gina – but we'll get together for a proper talk, very soon. And by the way, is your mother still looking for helpers?'

'Yes, she's having terrible trouble trying to start a committee. Shall I let you have our phone number?'

'Hey, Bart!' Don yelled, 'where's the key to the store-room? Flatfoot Fenella's just trodden on the last of the ping pong balls.'

'Coming –' Bart took the scribbled note Gina handed him, and hurried off.

The replacement balls were found, and she teamed up with Graham for a fast and furious game against Bart's girlfriend Carolyn and a boy called Roy. Carolyn seemed surprised anyone so young could hit the ball so hard. 'You'll be our secret weapon next time we play against a rival club, Gina,' she laughed. One way and another, it was a great evening.

The best moment of all came later though, when Gina was back home and getting ready for bed. Mum came dashing upstairs to tell her, 'Bart Ellis has just rung me. He sounds exactly the sort of person we need on the committee. Bags of enthusiasm, lovely sense of humour. Really, he's the answer to a prayer!'

Delighted, Gina thought, Tamsin's father reckons

God doesn't listen to prayers – but he certainly listened to Mum's! I may not be able to persuade Tamsin her father doesn't know what he's talking about, but I can at least tell her I don't want to listen to any more of his stupid so-called jokes. People don't like hearing their friends being made fun of – and Jesus is my friend. That's what I'll have to try and make her understand.

Chapter Five

'Any idea what Mum's up to?' Charlie asked after tea next day. Gina was struggling with a particularly difficult maths homework problem. She had already covered a whole page of paper with crossings-out.

'Isn't that her sewing machine I can hear? Maybe she's making her costume,' she told him, hoping that would be the end of the conversation. But no, he wanted to know more.

'Costume? What costume?'

'Just something she plans to wear next time she collects signatures for the petition, I think. You wouldn't be interested.'

'I might!' Charlie was back to his old game of contradicting everything his sister said. 'Why don't you call Mum down and ask her to show you where you're going wrong with that sum? Then I can sneak up to her room and take a look.'

'Charlie, NO!'

'All right.' He shrugged his shoulders. 'I'll tiptoe up there anyway and peep through the keyhole.'

'Mum's bedroom hasn't got a keyhole.'

'I know it hasn't, Frosty-face. I was only joking. Can't you tell the difference between when I'm joking and when I'm serious?'

'Not always, Charlie,' Gina admitted. Not lately at any rate, she thought. She could remember a time when he'd been a proper little giggler. She'd only had to creep up behind and tickle him, to set him off. He used to pester her to tell him elephant jokes – then collapse in a heap, halfway through trying to repeat them to Dad.

Nowadays though, if she mentioned some funny story that everyone in 2B was laughing at, he'd claim 'that's *ages* old'. She was sure too, that if she reached out to tickle him now, he'd push her away. The only times she saw him fooling around were when he and his friend Jacko were together.

'How about this?' Charlie said suddenly. He picked up the pen she'd been using, and scribbled a cartoon face over her crossed-out sums. Just an upturned, smiling mouth beneath two wide-open eyes, yet it looked tremendously like him.

'I'll hold it up, to let you know when I've said something funny, shall I?' he asked cheekily.

'Oh, you!' She aimed a punch that just stopped short of his nose. 'You're impossible!' But you're still my brother, she thought. And although she didn't put her appeal into words, Charlie seemed to know what was bothering her.

'Even if Mum's door did have a keyhole, I wouldn't feel right about using it. *You* know that. I expect she'll tell us soon, anyway.'

He was quite right. They only had to wait till Wednesday.

Neither of them stayed on after school that day. There weren't any practices for netball or hockey, so they walked home together, stopping off to buy a couple of ice lollies from a shop near the hospital.

'Look at those three cars, all the same make, driving along one after another,' Charlie said on his way out of the shop. 'The one in front has got some sort of flag on its bonnet. Where d'you reckon they're going?'

'They could be heading for St Saviour's,' Gina suggested. 'See that crowd outside the main entrance? Perhaps there's going to be some sort of ceremony. Let's go and watch.'

'Boring,' Charlie objected. He changed his mind though, once he'd caught sight of a dark green van, parked further down the road. 'That van's from our local radio station. They must be in on whatever's happening. Maybe I could see all their broadcasting stuff.'

The three cars pulled up right beside the waiting crowd. Out of them came half a dozen men and a woman dressed all in yellow with a hat like a pale yellow pancake. The first man had a gold chain with a medallion, hanging round his neck.

'That's the Mayor,' Charlie nudged Gina.

Going closer, Gina spotted several of the people in the crowd holding up SAVE ST SAVIOUR'S posters.

'Mum had those printed. She should be here somewhere,' she said.

'Maybe she's stuck behind that very tall bloke with the woolly hat on,' Charlie wondered.

The Mayor cleared his throat and began to speak.

'Ladies and gentlemen, I have with me today the members of the Finance Subcommittee. Their task is to visit all four outlying hospitals in this area – at Riversmeet, that is to say, at Hazelgrove, Middle Taynton, and in our own town of Upperleigh –'

'Get to the point!' the man in the woolly hat shouted.

'Their task,' the Mayor repeated, 'is to visit all four hospitals. They must then recommend which of the four should be closed, and which allowed to remain open.'

'But before they go one step further,' said a voice Gina recognised, 'they'll need to ask *my* permission!'

The people who'd been standing immediately in front of the hospital door shuffled sideways. Hidden behind them had been Mum. Now everybody could see that she was dressed up in the long green robes and fur trimmed hat of a Tudor merchant!

'So that's what she wanted the organ loft curtains for,'

Gina muttered. The green brocade hung in heavy folds, making Mum look very dignified.

'Never mind what she's wearing,' snapped Charlie, 'Look what she's got round her wrists. Chains!'

It was true. Mum had actually chained herself to the door handle, to stop the members of the Subcommittee from getting into the hospital.

'My name is Hal Whittinghame,' she explained. 'In 1576, I gave both land and money so that this hospital could be built. The life of my beloved son Edward had been saved by clever doctors and dedicated nursing – and I wanted the good people of Upperleigh to receive the same excellent care.'

Gina turned to whisper excitedly to Charlie, 'Hey! Mum's telling everybody the story that Mrs Stott told me.' But Charlie was scurrying away to the local radio van, and couldn't hear her.

The Mayor interrupted Mum.

'Very interesting. Very historical, no doubt. But hardly relevant to today's investigation, surely?' Already the members of the Subcommittee were starting to look impatient. The lady was having trouble holding on to her flat pancake hat in the breeze.

'I don't agree. The purpose of the investigation is to find out whether Upperleigh still needs its own local hospital,' Mum argued. 'And there's no need to go inside to find out, when the evidence is all around us. Everyone with me today will be in serious difficulties if St Saviour's is closed down!'

'She's right, Mister,' the woman standing next to Mum agreed. 'I can't afford to go to the City General every time my slipped disc plays up. Think of all the wages I'd lose!'

'And if my old dad is moved from the men's ward here, I'll only be able to visit him a couple of times a week. He's used to me coming in every time I get home from work. He'll fret. He's bound to, isn't he?' asked the man with the woolly hat.

A young woman wearing a bright purple jumpsuit was going round with a hand-held microphone to pick up what was being said. The Mayor shouldered his way forward and grabbed the microphone from her.

'We've wasted enough time,' he boomed. 'I really must ask you to unchain yourself, Madam.'

'She can't,' the man in the woolly hat announced smugly. 'The chains are padlocked, and I threw the key to the padlock down the nearest drain.'

'Oh, no!' gasped Gina.

Up to that point, she'd been enjoying the play-acting. She'd specially admired Mum's costume, which made her look like an oil painting come to life. Now though, it was clear from the dismay on Mum's face that the man hadn't warned her he planned to throw the key away.

'Wire cutters – we'll need wire cutters,' the Mayor announced pompously. He signalled to the uniformed driver from the car with the flag on its bonnet, ordering him to fetch them from the nearest hardware shop.

Gina saw Mum glance down at her wrists, as if she was worried the cutters might cut into them too. She tried to push nearer to where Mum was standing. The young woman in charge of the microphone was right in her way.

'Do you happen to know the name of the woman dressed up as Hal Whittinghame?' she asked. 'I'm sure our listeners would be interested.'

Speak into that mike? I can't! thought Gina. The inside of her mouth had gone dry, as it did whenever Tamsin made rude remarks about Jesus. But I can't let Mum down by being too scared to speak.

So, hoarsely, she managed to explain, 'Her name is Mrs Reed. She's my mum.'

'Really?' the local radio presenter prompted.

'Yes, and I think she's terrific,' Gina went on. 'There's

no-one ill in our family at the moment, thank goodness. She's fighting for St Saviour's to stay open, because of all the other people from Upperleigh who need looking after. I think that's great!'

People in the crowd began to clap. Gina caught sight of Mum smiling and mouthing a grateful 'Thanks'. The Mayor's driver came hurrying up. He was holding a set of keys.

'The hardware shop manager reckoned one of these should fit the padlock,' he told the Mayor.

Mum let out a great sigh of relief. Luckily the third key he tried released the chains. They fell to the pavement with a noisy clash.

'At last!' said the Mayor. The members of the Sub-committee followed him through the opened door, without looking in Mum's direction. The local radio presenter announced, 'The protest seems to be over now,' and walked back toward the green van.

Already, the people who'd been holding up posters were starting to drift away.

'No, wait!' called Mum. She looked down at Gina, who was crouching to pick up the chain. 'You didn't happen to see which way that silly man who threw the key away went, did you?'

''Fraid not, Mum.'

'He must have guessed I wanted a word with him. Of all the ridiculous things to do! I'd been planning to open the door as soon as I'd finished my speech, and lead the Mayor and his guests around the wards, still dressed as Hal Whittinghame. Just a little play-acting to cheer up the patients. They get awfully bored, having to lie in bed day after day.'

Taking her robes off, she added, 'It would have been useful to listen in on what the Subcommittee members were saying, too. I might have been able to pick up some hint as to which of the four hospitals has the most chance of staying open.'

'Never mind, Mum. That was a terrific speech you made. And how did you manage that hat?' Smiling, Mum explained.

'I took one of the four-cornered felt caps that the ladies wear in our church choir. I trimmed it with the fur collar from the winter coat you grew out of last year.'

'Brill!' approved Gina, trying the hat on for size.

Still chatting, they began to head for home.

'What about those chains around your wrists?'

'I took the security chain off Charlie's bike. He won't be best pleased when he finds the key's missing. Where's he got to, anyway?'

Gina looked round in surprise.

'He wanted to speak to the people in the radio van – ask to see their equipment. I suppose once they left, he decided to hurry home and start getting the tea ready.'

'Machines and food? You're right, they seem to be all he's interested in these days,' Mum agreed. 'But I shouldn't complain. His form teacher is very pleased with the results he's been getting. And it's good for a boy his age to have such a healthy appetite. Unlike you, Miss Lanky-legs, he's still got a lot of growing to do.'

They turned in at the gate to Number 23, noticing that Charlie had left the front door open, and his anorak had ended up on the floor as usual.

'He's headed straight for the pantry,' guessed Mum.

For once though, she was wrong. Charlie was in the front room, on the phone to his dad in Sheffield.

'Dad,' he was saying, 'you've got to get back here straight away! Last I saw of Mum, she'd chained herself to the door of St Saviour's Hospital. She's probably locked up in prison by now!'

Chapter Six

Mum was absolutely furious.

'Charlie!' she shouted, coming in from the hall at the run, to snatch the phone from his hand.

'Still there, Bob?' she asked Dad. 'Good. I hope you weren't too bothered by that nonsense Charlie was talking, because there's not a word of truth in it. For a start, nobody called the police – as Charlie would have known if he hadn't been so busy running off to tell tales – *Wait! Where do you think you're off to, now?*'

She let the receiver drop, muttering 'You talk to your father, Gina,' and went chasing after Charlie. He was already storming out of the house, slamming the front door behind him. Gina could hear her father calling 'What's going on?' at the other end of the line – he sounded very far away. Her hands were shaking as she tried to answer.

'Dad, is that you? Dad, everything's fine, really it is. Mum had this clever idea that she'd dress up as the founder of St Saviour's Hospital. She made a speech to the people who'd come to decide whether it should be kept open. Ever such a good speech.'

There was a laugh from the other end of the line.

'Your mother was always keen on amateur dramatics. In fact she was acting in a play the first time I saw her. Even so, Gina, I don't like the sound of her actually chaining herself to the hospital door.'

Gina hesitated. The last thing she wanted was for Dad

to come home and tell Mum she must give up her fight to save St Saviour's. Still, she didn't want him to be too angry with Charlie, either.

'I was worried too, when I saw what was going on,' she admitted. 'So I can't blame Charlie for getting in a bit of a panic. But honestly, Mum was planning to take the chains off, once she'd finished her speech. Only she couldn't, because some silly man threw the padlock key away.'

'PAGING MR REED. PAGING MR REED. WILL MR REED PLEASE COME TO THE SECURITY OFFICE DIRECTLY,' requested a metallic voice in faraway Sheffield.

'I've got to hang up now, Gina,' Dad said hurriedly. 'You can tell your mum I'll be ringing her tonight from my digs, once I've had a quick sandwich and a coffee. As for Charlie, better remind him not to contact me at work unless there's a *real* emergency. Love to you all.'

Then he was gone. Gina breathed a sigh of relief. I hope there isn't too much of a shouting match when Mum catches up with Charlie, she thought. The afternoon was ending. Crossing to the window to pull the curtains, she saw her mum and her brother standing on the street corner. They were glaring at one another, their angry faces spotlit by the harsh yellow streetlamp light.

Later, at teatime, she was handing round plates of Welsh Rarebit when she heard a knock on the door. Opening up, she found that Graham Stott had come round to see her.

'I could come back later, if you're all eating,' he suggested, looking at her oven glove. 'I just thought this might be a good time to come and see some old photos that Gran's found –'

'Of St Saviour's? Great!' It took Gina no more than a moment to decide she'd far sooner get out of the house than spend the evening listening to Charlie's grumbles and Mum's hard-done-by sighs. 'It won't take me long to finish the snack I was having – and there's plenty of tea in the pot if you'd like a cup. Then we could go round to your gran's place.'

'Fine,' he agreed.

The old lady made the two of them very welcome. She had turned her gas fire full on, so that her room was almost oven hot.

'I'd prefer a real fire, of course. Still, can you imagine me pottering to and from the coal shed, with a bucket dangling from my walking frame? Pretty ridiculous, I'd look.'

Gina was impressed by the way she was able to make fun of the situation. I'm not sure I could, if I had arthritis, she thought.

Graham wandered across to pick up a fat photo album with a faded blue cover which he'd spotted on the windowsill.

'Are the pictures you want Gina to see in here, Gran?' he asked.

'That's right. You'll find them towards the back. No point in showing her the early years where I'm dressed in my Sunday best, being handed piano prizes.'

But Gina turned the pages slowly.

'All those silver cups,' she marvelled. 'You must have been terrifically talented.'

'More likely, I was a terrific show-off,' was the smiling answer.

Several pages further on, the theme of the snapshots began to change.

'Look, Graham. That's one of the main wards at St Saviour's,' Gina pointed out.

'Now you're getting there. That's me in the old fashioned uniform, pushing the medicine trolley. The men in the beds are all wounded airmen.'

Graham said, 'They look pretty cheerful. But – what was the matter with the bloke whose head was covered in bandages?'

'Facial burns. He'd been pulled out from a Spitfire that caught fire after it crashed,' Mrs Stott remembered, grimly. Impatiently she added, 'but the snap I particularly want Gina to see was taken in the grounds of the hospital, when most of the airmen were convalescing.'

'This one?'

'That's right. Take it out from the album, will you? There should be some writing on the back.' The message had been written with a scratchy pen in blue-black ink. After almost fifty years it was faded, and difficult to make out.

Gina peered closely.

'*To our very own chirpy Birdie*,' she read aloud. '*From the lads of 522 Squadron. Ginger – Spud – Dusty Miller.* Then there are two or three I can't make any sense of. It's signed by a Squadron Leader, though. Gavin Murdoch? Would that be his name?'

'That's it. That's the man,' Graham's gran agreed. 'Now what I've been wondering is this. Do you think you could trace him, by writing to the RAF ex-servicemen's association? If he knew St Saviour's was in trouble, I'm sure he'd like to help in any way he could.'

Turning the photograph over, Gina looked at the smiling men in their long plaid dressing gowns, posing under a centuries-old mulberry tree in the hospital garden.

'Is he the one with the huge moustache?' she asked.

'How did you guess?'

'I'm not sure. Except that he looks in charge, somehow.'

'Oh, he was,' the old lady remembered. 'He wouldn't let any of the others feel too sorry for themselves. Not even the poor boy who was learning to walk again with the help of an artificial leg.'

'Then I'd certainly like to try and find him,' Gina decided. 'He sounds the sort of person Mum needs to back her up.'

'If you succeed, tell him Birdie still remembers the lads from 522, will you?' Mrs Stott murmured drowsily. Her head was drooping, eyelids slowly shuttering over her eyes.

'Time we were off,' whispered Graham. 'I'll see you home.' Gina nodded her thanks. Mum will be pleased he didn't expect me to cut through the backstreets on my own, she thought.

On her way home from school next day, she called in at the Public Library.

'Have you got a reference book that lists the addresses of ex-servicemen's associations, please?' she asked. The girl at the desk found the booklet she needed, and showed her how to photocopy the information she was looking for.

That meant there was just time to pop into the Post Office before it closed.

'One stamp please – no, I mean two,' said Gina, thinking she ought to send a stamped addressed envelope for a reply.

'First, or second class?'

The sooner her letter arrived, the better.

'First, I suppose.' She counted the pocket money left in her purse. It seemed to be disappearing much faster than usual. And Tamsin's birthday was only a few days away. Hadn't she been planning to buy a really special present?

Back at Number 23, she started rummaging through the drawers in the Welsh dresser.

'Any idea where Mum keeps her writing paper, Charlie?'

'Same drawer you're looking in. I doubt if she's got any left though. *So* many important letters about St Saviour's to write,' he said – mimicking the way Mum's voice sounded when she talked to posh grown-ups.

'Well, Great Aunt Norah sent you notelets for Christmas, didn't she? As a cunning hint that you ought to send more thank-you letters? Could you let me have a couple of those?'

'Only if you promise not to use them for anything to do with that soppy old hospital,' Charlie muttered.

'I can't –'

'Buy them off me then. Fifteen pence each –'

'My last thirty pence. You're a mean pig, Charlie Reed!' said Gina, as she handed the money over.

Mum was late getting back from her latest meeting.

'You've no idea what a difference the publicity we got from the local radio has made,' she told Gina excitedly. 'The hall was packed, absolutely packed. We had a tremendous brainstorming session, and you're never going to guess what idea I came up with, to win even more support. Where's Charlie by the way?'

'Gone to bed.'

'Already?' Mum looked at her watch. 'Heavens! Is that the time? My news had better wait till morning then – if I keep you up till all hours chatting, you'll be falling asleep in class tomorrow.'

Tibby was snoring noisily on Gina's lap. She dislodged him as gently as she could, unfastening the claw he'd hooked in her skirt. After one wheezy grunt of protest, he settled down to snooze again on the sofa.

Wish I was a cat like him, Gina thought, once she'd climbed into bed. Waiting up for Mum, she'd reached that awful stage where she was so tired, sleep was slow in coming. And there was a niggling little worry to share with Jesus, too.

'Please, Jesus,' she prayed, 'Don't let Mum's latest idea be *too* over the top. A few of the girls gave me some very funny looks in class today, because they'd heard how she'd chained herself to the hospital door. You do understand don't you, Jesus? I don't want them saying she's gone completely potty.'

In the morning though, when she heard what Mum had in mind, there was a moment when she wondered if Jesus had even been listening?

'Mum –' she protested, 'You don't mean you want me to –'

'You won't be on your own,' Mum chipped in, 'I've already rounded up ten volunteers. And I thought maybe that nice boy who brought you home from his grandmother's the other evening might like to come along, to make the numbers up to a round dozen.'

'Mum, no! I wouldn't dare ask Graham.'

'Tamsin, then?'

'*Definitely* not Tamsin!'

She heard Charlie snigger. The milk from his cornflakes sputtered all over the kitchen table.

'And you've already refused, I suppose?'

'Course I have. Why don't you?'

Mum at once looked hurt.

'Believe me, Gina, I don't want to steam-roller you into doing anything you wouldn't feel comfortable with. Anyway there's no need to make your mind up here and now. Just let me know by Friday, so I can work out how many wellington boots I'll need to adapt.'

'Wellington boots!' Charlie snorted.

I'm between the two of them again, Gina thought. But this time the game isn't piggy in the middle. It feels more like tug of war. She thought how chuffed Charlie would be if she sided with him for a change. Besides, if Tamsin and the others laughed at Mum's latest stunt, she'd be able to claim 'I wasn't in on it.'

Where would that leave Mum, though? She'd have those ten volunteers – still, that wasn't the same as family backing, was it? What was the point of going on local radio to say 'Mum's ideas are great,' but then refusing to go along with them?

Cautiously, she asked, 'That man in the woolly hat isn't coming, is he?'

'No,' Mum laughed. 'He's keeping his distance, because he knows I'm still cross about what he did. Bart Ellis is keen to get involved though. He's probably bringing his girlfriend.'

So it wasn't just people of Mum's own age, who'd agreed to help out?

'All right. Count me in,' she decided, gathering up her homework books so she didn't have to see the face Charlie was pulling.

She sat next to Carolyn on Saturday, to watch the first half of a home match between Upperleigh Rangers and Riversmeet United.

'I'd be enjoying this more if I didn't keep thinking about what your mum wants us to do at half time,' Carolyn confided.

'Really? I thought it was only me who had the jitters.'

'Oh, I expect I'll be all right when we get out onto the pitch. If I'm with Bart, I can do all sorts of things I'd never have dreamed of doing alone,' Carolyn explained. Bart was sitting on Carolyn's other side. He was completely involved in the game, yelling 'Offside! Offside!'

Gina said, 'It's like that when I'm with Mum. I don't feel so small – and I don't get that horrible feeling that everyone's staring at me.'

'That's because you love her, I expect,' Carolyn said. 'Being with people we love gives us confidence, I reckon –' She blushed brick red. She must mean she loves Bart. I wonder if they'll get engaged? thought Gina.

The half-time whistle blew.

'That's our cue,' called Mum. She led the way onto the pitch. All the eleven people coming on after her, Gina included, looked as if they were limping.

The crowd on the terraces stared. There were cheers and hoots as the 'accident victims' paraded around the pitch. Each had what looked like a right leg in plaster.

Really though, they were all wearing tall white wellington boots on their right legs. The boots had been stiffened with wooden rulers, taped to the insides.

Mum spoke through a loud hailer.

'By the time this interval is over, I want to see my friends' boots smothered in signatures. The signatures will be added to the thousands we've already collected, asking that St Saviour's Hospital should remain open. Remember – IF OUR LOCAL HOSPITAL CLOSES, NONE OF US WILL HAVE A LEG TO STAND ON!'

Chapter Seven

For once on Monday, it was Gina who had something exciting to tell Tamsin, and not the other way round.

'So there we were,' she said, 'leaving the terraces with masses of signatures scrawled on our boots – when Luke Keenan came out from the players' dressing room.'

'Luke Keenan?' Tamsin repeated.

'Yes, he's Upperleigh Rangers' star striker, didn't you know?' Too late, Gina remembered seeing a poster with the young footballer's craggy, good looking face smiling down from the wall above Tamsin's bed.

'Of all the mean, underhand, stinking tricks,' Tamsin spat out. 'You didn't tell me you'd be going to the match on Saturday, did you? You didn't invite me to come with you?'

'But Tamsin, you've said all along you're not interested in Mum's petition.'

'Of course I'm not interested. *Nobody's* interested.'

'Luke Keenan was,' put in Brenda. The two girls turned to stare at her. Why's she got that peculiar smile on her face, Gina wondered? Angrily, Tamsin demanded, 'How do you know?'

'My brother Stuart is an Upperleigh Rangers supporter,' Brenda explained. 'He saw Luke Keenan tell Gina all about the cartilage trouble he'd been having, and the terrific repair job which one of the St Saviour's docs has done to his knee. And then he saw Luke actually sign the boot she was wearing.'

'If I'd been there, I could have got his autograph, too! That's why you kept quiet about where you were going,' claimed Tamsin. 'You were jealous, Gina Reed. Rotten jealous, just because Brenda and I had such a great time together at Green Acres. You've been waiting for a chance to get even with me for inviting her, ever since I came back.'

'Of course I haven't,' Gina protested. She knew very well that the 'good time' Tamsin was talking about had mostly consisted of listening to Brenda's moans. Now though, the two of them were walking away together, arms around one anothers' shoulders.

'I don't know if you'd be interested, Tamsin,' Brenda was saying, 'but Stuart took a video recorder to the quarter finals last year, when Luke Keenan scored those three brill goals against Norham City. You could come to my house to tea tonight, if you wanted to watch the video he made.'

Brenda's never had a proper friend of her own, Gina realised. She'll do everything she can to make trouble between me and Tamsin, in the hopes that Tamsin will give up spending time with me, and go around with her instead. Tamsin's got no patience with her, really – but so long as she thinks I'll feel miserable seeing the two of them together, she'll go on *pretending* to like her.

Left alone, Gina wandered toward the chain link fence that separated her school from the Junior school that Charlie went to. She could see a mass of Juniors racing about at the end of lunch break. They seemed to be re-enacting the chase scene from last night's episode of 'Americops'.

'I'm comin' to get ya, Punk! Da-da-da-da –'

'Yeeeeargh!'

There was no sign of Charlie or his friend Jacko – no, wait! Wasn't that them, climbing over the wall on the far side of the Junior school grounds? They're bunking off, she thought. But there was no way she could go after them, without making herself late for afternoon lessons. Anyway, by the time she made her way round to the stretch of main road that backed on to the wall, they'd be long gone.

So far as she knew, Charlie had never played truant before. Most likely it was Jacko who'd dared him into going. She didn't know much about him, because his family had only recently moved into the district. Mum usually tried to keep track of the boys Charlie went around with; it was only because she'd been busy with the fight to keep St Saviour's open that she hadn't checked up this time, Gina thought.

She spent the whole afternoon worrying about what the two boys might be doing, while they should have been in class. She was expecting Mum to be worried, when Charlie didn't arrive home with her. Instead, Mum smiled and said, 'Jacko's mother just phoned, to tell me Charlie would be staying to tea at their house. Such a nice lady, she sounded. By the way, Gina, do you think you could address some envelopes for me, before you start out for the youth club this evening?'

There was no point in mentioning her suspicions while Mum was only half listening, Gina thought, as she went to sit opposite Mum at the kitchen table and copy addresses from a printed list onto one brown envelope after another. It could have been two other boys I saw, anyway – and besides, I hate telling tales.

For tea, she and Mum shared some rather stale sponge cake, and finished off the last broken bits from a pack of chocolate chip biscuits.

'I expect I'll be able to fit the food shopping in tomorrow,' Mum promised, vaguely.

When she reached the youth club, Graham and Don were standing outside, staring at the notice board.

'See this, Gina?' Graham asked. 'Is it one of the posters that your mum has been putting up? Only someone's been mucking around with it.'

'Mucking around? Oh, no!'

Over the neat printed slogan UPPERLEIGH NEEDS ITS LOCAL HOSPITAL, was spray painted the single vivid scarlet comment RUBBISH!

'We saw three more posters about St Saviour's on our way here,' Don added, 'and they'd all been scrawled over.'

'Which – which way did you come?' Gina could hardly get the words out, for fear of what the answer might be.

'Same as usual,' Don explained casually. 'I live in a flat over the car showrooms on the main road. We cut through the alleyway at the side of the showrooms, and crossed the railway bridge.'

It was Graham who noticed how all the colour had drained from Gina's face once she heard that.

'Hey! Has Don given you a clue as to who might have messed your mum's posters up?' he guessed.

'I'm just feeling a bit sick, that's all,' Gina told him, using that as an excuse to race for the ladies' toilet at the back of the hall. She might have avoided answering his question fair and square, but she wasn't lying. Her insides felt as if someone with a cold hard hand had made a sudden grab at them.

The route Don described led straight from where she'd seen two boys bunking off from the Junior school grounds, to the hall where the youth club meetings were held. The scarlet spray-paint was another possible clue. Hadn't Charlie told her that Jacko planned to paint his new model plane bright scarlet?

Carolyn came in and found her at the sink, splashing cold water on her face.

'Graham says you've got a touch of the colly-wobbles. Would you like me to take you home?' she offered.

If I say 'yes', Gina thought, I won't have to answer any more awkward questions. No, she realised, I'm not thinking straight. If I get back from the club early,

Mum's bound to want to know why. She'll be the one asking the questions, then. And how can I tell her anything, till I've at least *tried* to get some sense out of Charlie?

She grabbed a paper towel, hoping Carolyn wouldn't notice she was wiping tears as well as tapwater from her cheeks.

'Thanks, but I think I'd rather sit quiet for a while.'

'All right, if you're sure.'

Bart was trying to teach the club members how to play badminton that evening. There were screams of laughter as one by one they discovered that a badminton shuttle behaves in a very different way from a ping-pong ball. Gina watched from the sidelines, joining in the laughter whenever she thought someone might be looking in her direction.

How can I ask Charlie if he sneaked away from school so he could paint rude remarks all over the posters that Mum's so proud of, she was wondering? And what can I do, if he says 'yes'? The badminton session ended at last, and Gina accepted a lift home in Bart's minibus. After she'd waved goodbye to him and Carolyn, she let herself in at the front door – and walked in on a tremendous row between Mum and Charlie.

'Of course it wasn't Jacko's idea,' Charlie was yelling, 'It was *my* idea!'

The two of them were facing one another across the kitchen table, with a SAVE ST SAVIOUR'S poster between them. Scrawled in scarlet across the poster was the question WHY BOTHER?

'So – these initials – C.R –' Mum was saying slowly.

'Yeah, they're mine. Graffiti artists always sign their own work.'

'You're not going to tell me you think of yourself as an *artist*?' Mum demanded.

'Why not?' Charlie challenged her. 'Our art teacher reckons paintings need to make statements. And my statement is, if people have to go to hospital, they ought to go to a proper *modern* hospital.'

He was working himself up, his face flushed, his words blurted out like sobs. 'In a modern hospital, a man who was really, really ill would have a hundred more chances to get better – a thousand more chances –' He pushed past Gina. She and Mum could hear him racing upstairs to his bedroom and slamming the door.

'It's just a temper tantrum, Mum. Like when he was a baby,' said Gina.

Mum sounded more tired than angry.

'When he was a baby,' she said, 'I knew what was causing the tantrums. He was screaming because he'd got a new tooth coming through, or because I was late changing his nappy.' She crumpled the scrawled-over poster into an untidy ball and squashed it down hard into the pedal bin.

'What I don't understand this time, is why our fight to keep the hospital open seems so *wrong* to him? I don't expect him to agree with everything I do – but he's made his disagreement so public.'

Flopping down heavily into a kitchen chair, she explained, 'One of our neighbours brought this poster to show me, Gina. According to her, Charlie and Jacko were standing near the hoarding it was on, tossing their spray can between them, as if they were hoping she'd notice them. And this was during school hours, so they must have been playing truant.'

'Perhaps they were just showing off,' Gina suggested. Mum shook her head.

'Nice of you to try and cheer me up, but I think there's more to it than that. Perhaps I should find someone else to take over the organisation of the Save St Saviour's campaign? Your dad has had to spend so much time in Sheffield, lately. Maybe Charlie thinks we're both neglecting him?'

'But that's no excuse for being so nasty to you, Mum!'

Gina protested. She went upstairs and called through Charlie's door, 'You can't hide in there for ever! Come down and say you're sorry, and you'll never be so stupid and beastly to Mum again!'

She waited and waited. But all she could hear from the bedroom was a series of loud and obviously fake snores.

Chapter Eight

Charlie arrived at breakfast next morning with his stereo headphones on, so he wouldn't have to talk to Mum. Gina hardly noticed. She was reading a letter which the postman had put through the letter box while she was on her way downstairs.

'Dear Miss Reed,' she read out loud, 'the Association passed your query directly to me, rather than waste time sending you my address. I was most concerned to hear of plans to close St Saviour's – the hospital where I was patched up so marvellously after I crashed my Spitfire in 1942.

Your friend Mrs Stott, (or Birdie, as we used to call her – and what a treat it was to learn that our dear Birdie is still chirping!) is quite right in thinking I would be opposed to such a scheme. I shall write to my Member of Parliament, making my views on the subject crystal clear.

However, I feel that a more personal involvement in your fight to keep the grand old hospital open would prove more effective in the long run. Perhaps your mother could let me have a list of the further protests she plans to make, and the dates for each of them? We RAF types never like to go against the enemy until we've received a thorough briefing!

Yours most sincerely,

Gavin Murdoch, Wing Cmdr, (Retd).'

'Wing Commander, mmh? That's a step up from

Squadron Leader,' Mum explained. 'He must have been promoted after he came out of hospital. He sounds just the sort of man I need to advise me on tactics, doesn't he?'

'Then you'll send him the list that he asked for?'

'Yes, certainly. I've got a mass of washing to do, but once it's in the machine, I'll get my writing things out. He's going to want to know about our march through Upperleigh with the Silver Band – did I tell you I'd got their bandmaster to agree to that? But first there'll be our Sponsored Bed Push. You don't think he'll be offended if I enclose a sponsorship form, do you?'

'I don't know what you're on about, Mum. This is the first I've heard about any – did you say Bed Push?'

Mum nodded, looking vaguely flustered.

'Surely I must have mentioned going to ask the local police for permission? And then there was the insurance I had to take out, in case anyone on the team is involved in an accident – you *can't* not have heard how much I was charged –'

'Mum, honestly, I'm completely in the dark. What bed are the police allowing what team to push, and where will they be pushing it to?'

'Well, honestly! I do think you could work the answers out for yourself, if you'd only use your imagination. The bed belongs to St Saviour's, the team will be made up from my Save St Saviour's volunteers, and the route will go all the way from St Saviour's front entrance to the City General Hospital!'

Of course, Gina's name joined Mum's on the list of volunteers. So when Tamsin announced to the class, a day or so later, 'My parents are letting me have a birthday disco this year, with a light show and all the latest hits,' her first question was, 'When will it be?'

She couldn't help noticing Brenda Tomlin's sly smile, as Tamsin answered.

'Um, we couldn't book the DJ for my actual birthday.

And anyway, my mother reckoned more of my friends would be free to turn up on a Saturday afternoon.'

'Great idea,' Brenda agreed, 'Practically everybody is free on Saturdays.'

Practically everybody except me, you mean, thought Gina, bitterly. The words were on the tip of her tongue. Seeing how narrowly Brenda seemed to be watching her though, she clamped her mouth shut and walked away.

Tamsin's mother had nothing to do with the timing, she reasoned. Knowing I've spent all my Saturdays lately helping Mum, *Brenda* persuaded Tamsin to hold the disco on a day when I wouldn't be able to go. It's all part of her plan to take my place as Tamsin's special friend.

At first, Gina felt so angry that she wanted to do something that would make Brenda feel as miserable as she herself had been made to feel. Gradually though, she calmed down. She thought about Jesus, who had loved his enemies, even though they'd plotted to have him killed. He'd understood the reasons why they had acted the way they did. Shouldn't she be trying to understand poor lonely Brenda?

A couple of days later however, an invitation to the birthday disco turned up in her locker. Mrs Gerard had arranged for them to be specially printed, on crinkle edged card with gold lettering.

COME TO MY DISCO PARTY!
2pm to 6pm
SATURDAY
RSVP

Underneath, in her own handwriting, Tamsin had scrawled '*I really want you to be there, Gina.*'

Now what shall I do, wondered Gina? Needing time to be alone with Jesus, she volunteered to take a set of playbooks, which Form 2B had finished with, back to

61

the school's Book Store.

The huge walk-in cupboard, with its row upon row of metal shelving, was an odd place to pray in. Still, for as long as she could remember she'd known there was no need to wait for a special place, or speak in special old-fashioned words. So she told Jesus simply, 'Mum's quite keen for me to take part in the Bed Push – but I've helped her so much with her other stunts, I'm sure she'd say "Enjoy yourself, for once", if I showed her Tamsin's invitation. And really, I'm awfully tempted.'

For a moment, the arguments against joining Mum on Saturday came crowding into her mind. Tamsin would be thrilled. Brenda would be furious, and serve her right! Charlie would say 'about time, too.' And anyway, there'd probably be so many volunteers that Mum would hardly notice she wasn't there.

But that word 'tempted' stopped her in her tracks.

'Jesus,' she asked quietly, 'did you feel like I do now, when you were in the wilderness, and the Devil tried to persuade you to do things *his* way? I know that was a much more important temptation than the one I'm facing, of course. Still, Tamsin is trying to get me to break my promise to Mum, isn't she?'

In the silence of the Book Store, Gina thought about loyalty to Mum, to help with the fight to keep St Saviour's open, and to Jesus, whose commandments were 'Love God' and 'Love your neighbour as yourself.' The sick people who needed a hospital right on their doorstep in Upperleigh were her neighbours, weren't they?

'Thank you, Jesus,' she prayed. 'Once I've talked to you, I don't have to hear your answer in actual words, do I? You help me work it out for myself.' She looked up as a prefect came in to ask suspiciously, 'Have you got permission to be in here?'

'Yes,' Gina nodded. She put the last playbook up on the DRAMA shelf. 'But I'm going back to the classroom now, because I've finished what I came to do.'

That Saturday, she woke to find Mum in her bedroom, staring out of the window.

'After all my plans,' Mum was saying gloomily, '*now* look what's happened!'

Joining her at the window, Gina saw that the houses across the road had disappeared behind a wall of fog.

'Perhaps the wind will clear the fog away before our Bed Push starts,' she suggested.

'Wind? What wind?' Mum demanded.

Outside, the fog hung motionless, like a soggy grey blanket on some huge washing line. Charlie came out of the bathroom, grinning. He'd got up extra early because Mum had arranged for him to stay the whole day at Jacko's house, and he was in a hurry to get going. Any other Saturday, nothing less than an earthquake would have shifted him out of bed before nine.

'Seen the weather? You'll have to cancel today's stunt, won't you?' he asked.

'No,' Mum told him. 'Remember, our route is the same one that an ambulance would need to drive along if St Saviour's was closed, and somebody from Upperleigh needed emergency treatment. Those ambulancemen wouldn't stay home because of the fog, and neither shall I.'

'You'd better rig fog lamps on the bed, then,' claimed Charlie.

Gina thought, he and Mum will be shouting at one another again in a moment. Mum's bound to tell him not to be daft. Instead though, Mum went out onto the landing to give him a hug.

'Charlie Reed, that idea could be a lifesaver! Fog-lamps, eh? You're the one with the practical knowhow – have you got any idea how we could fix them up?'

Startled, Charlie protested, 'I was only joking.' Already however, Gina could see that the problem was starting to interest him.

'We'll use your bed to practise on,' he told her bossily,

and hurried downstairs, two steps at a time.

He was back before his sister had quite finished dressing. She tugged on her warmest sweater and popped her head out through the polo neck to watch what he was doing.

'Look,' he said, 'I've taken the torch with the extra strong beam from the garage. I'll wire it to one leg at the front end of the bed. You'd better buy another torch just like it, to use as your second headlamp.'

Slowly and carefully, he secured the torch to the bedleg, then flicked on the switch.

'That's going to show up good and bright, as you push the bed along,' he said.

'Fine,' Gina agreed, 'But we'll need red warning lights for the back of the bed as well, won't we? That's what a car or a lorry has, when the weather is as rotten as this.'

'Ta-raaa!' Charlie produced the battery operated rear light that belonged to his bike, taking it out from his pyjama pocket with a conjuror's grin. 'You'll have to buy a second one of these as well,' he told Mum. 'The man at the cycle shop sells them. And why don't you ask him if he can kit your bed-pushers out in day-glo belts, like the one I wear when I'm cycling after dark?'

This is great, Gina thought. If he hadn't agreed to spend the day with Jacko, I almost think we could have persuaded him to join our team today. It was one of those times – and they'd been all too rare, recently – when she was glad she had a brother.

'Definitely a three-sausage solution to our problems, that's what you've come up with,' Mum told him. 'Let's all have a really mammoth breakfast before we get going, shall we?'

Chapter Nine

It was after ten by the time Gina and Mum reached St Saviour's. Waiting for them in Reception were two young nurses, one tall and slim, the other more dumpy.

'You've been working so hard to keep our hospital going, Mrs Reed. We thought it was time we did our bit,' they explained.

'Of course, we could get jobs at some other hospital if St Saviour's had to shut down, but we love working here. The place is small enough for everyone to know one another by name, nurses *and* patients.'

They wheeled out the hospital bed which was ready for the Bed Push. Mum told them about Charlie's bright idea for equipping it with makeshift lights.

'Look, it's got taller legs than my bed,' Gina noticed. 'That's handy, isn't it? We'll be able to fix the torches at the same height as car headlights.'

Cathy, the taller of the two nurses, hurried away while the lights were being fixed. She came back with the biggest hospital nightgown she'd been able to find.

'This is for our patient to wear.'

'Oh, we'll take turns at being the patient,' Mum told her. 'I'm sure we'll be grateful for a lie-down every so often.'

They watched a familiar minibus park outside.

'Good, Bart's arrived,' said Mum, 'Go and ask him whether he managed to check the mileage, will you, Gina?' The answer came as a shock. Bart, who was wearing yellow waterproofs and hiking boots, announced that a diversion had been set up between Purford and Kettleby.

'That puts an extra two miles on our route. We're in for a ten mile hike, I'm afraid.'

Meanwhile the Reception phone was ringing. The girl at the desk called across to Mum, 'Apparently Mr and Mrs Weatherby won't be joining you today, Mrs Reed. Mr Weatherby has a sore throat, and his wife's decided to stay home and look after him.'

The second nurse, Roxanne, remembered, 'I took another call earlier, from a Miss Peebles. She won't be along till the fog clears.'

'But we can't wait any longer. We mustn't be late reaching the City General Hospital,' Mum explained. 'I've arranged for our local MP to meet us there. Besides, there'll be newspapermen taking photographs of our arrival. Day-glo belts on, everybody. We're on our way!'

With Cathy as patient, they wheeled the bed out through the main door. The fog had begun to lift, only to be replaced by a steady drizzle.

'I *was* rather hoping we'd have a crowd of well-wishers to see us off. The weather's put paid to that, though,' Mum murmured.

'Not to worry,' Roxanne told her. 'Look, the patients in the Men's Day Room are waving goodbye from their window.'

Gina was used to pushing the next door neighbours' baby in his pram, so she hadn't been expecting problems with the Bed Push. But as she peered through the bedrails, she could see all the cars and lorries coming in the opposite direction. Surely they were moving much too fast?

One angry motorist wound down his window to yell at them.

'What do you lot think you're playing at? I could have run you down!'

'Mum,' Gina whispered, 'I'm scared.'

'Swap places with me, then,' Mum suggested kindly. 'You'll feel safer, the closer you are to the kerb.'

Even after she'd moved, Gina didn't feel right.

'It's not just me I'm scared for, it's all of us,' she tried to explain.

There was a shriek of airbrakes as a lorry sped by with the driver bellowing, 'You lot! You ought to be locked up!'

Mum looked past Gina and Roxanne to Bart, who'd taken up position closest to the oncoming traffic.

'Are we really causing a traffic hazard, do you think?' she asked anxiously.

'Speaking as a driver myself, I've seen worse,' he told her. 'The police would never have given you permission to use this road, if they hadn't checked the safety aspects. And Charlie's makeshift lights give the other traffic plenty of warning that we're coming. I'm afraid drivers are simply in a bad mood because of the filthy weather. We're getting the backlash.'

'Don't you mean back-splash?' joked Cathy. 'This nightgown was white when we set out. With all the mudsplatters, it's more a speckled grey, now.' Gina was only half-listening. I could have been with Tamsin by now, helping her to get ready for this afternoon's disco party, she was thinking. And instead, it's Brenda that's gone round to her house. I expect they're up in Tamsin's bedroom together, with a mass of Tamsin's clothes spread out all over the bed, so's she can decide what to wear.

I enjoyed helping Mum when there were just the two of us, she remembered. And at the football match, I had Carolyn to talk to. She's older than me but not *that* much older. I don't want to spend a whole day plodding along like this though, with nobody taking any notice of me. Boring, boring, boring!

'I'm getting cold, lying here,' Cathy complained a

while later. 'Do you want to swap places with me, Rox-anne?'

'That's a point,' said Bart. 'We ought to work out how long a rest each of us gets on the bed.'

'Let's make each lie-down last fifteen minutes, shall we?' Mum suggested. 'Roxanne can go next, then Gina. Then you, Bart –'

'No, you. Ladies first!' Bart insisted. In the mean-while, Cathy had slipped off the bed. She was helping Roxanne pull the damp, muddy nightgown over her head.

With Roxanne on board, Gina thought, the bed was much harder to push. Her shoulders began to ache. She was hunched forward at an awkward angle, her eyes half closed, wishing Roxanne had gone on a diet before the Bed Push started.

Just then Bart announced, 'Here's where Purford Hill gets *really* steep,' and she realised it must be the hill, and not Roxanne, that was making her feel so uncomfort-able. A joker on a motor scooter overtook them.

'Run out of petrol, have you?' he called, 'Need a tow?'

What I need is more breath, thought Gina. Her throat was raw from the huge gulps of air she was having to take.

'Stop, everybody!' called Bart. 'We'll take the hill in three stages.' Which must mean there were two more stages, each as beastly steep as the one they had already climbed. It seemed to Gina that they'd hardly stopped any time at all before Bart gave the order, 'Right. On we go.'

'Slave driver,' giggled Cathy. It was all right for her to laugh, she'd only just left the bed. *Her* legs hadn't had time to feel the way Gina's felt – as if there was an elastic band stretching from her knee to her ankle, and somebody was tugging on it, hard.

On they pushed, and on again. At last, Purford village came into view.

'See that yellow road sign, just before the start of the main street?' Bart asked. 'That marks the turn-off to the diversion I warned you about.' Mum told him how glad she was that he'd scouted the route in advance.

'I'd have been worried sick if we'd come across the diversion sign and not known where it was leading to. There's a maze of lanes in the Pur valley, and a lot of them end up in farmyards.'

They began to move downhill. Now the bed seemed to want to go faster than they did, like a huge clumsy dog tugging at its leash. I'll have to let go of this bedrail soon, Gina thought. But when Mum turned to ask, 'Are you feeling all right,' she didn't want the others to think they'd made a mistake, including someone as young as she was on the team. So she just said, 'Fine.'

Luckily, just after they'd turned into the country lane, Roxanne swapped places with her, and gave her a chance to lie on the bed.

'We've knocked three miles off our total,' Bart announced. Gina lay back with her eyes closed, and shuddered. Seven more miles before they reached the City General? Could they really manage to push the bed that far?

Several minutes later, the bed began to judder and shake.

'Hey! What are you pushing me over *now*?' Gina asked, as her eyes jolted open.

'Cattle-grid. So much for my skills as a path finder,' Bart said, grinning. 'I've missed a turning and led you onto one of those farmyard dead ends that your mum was talking about, earlier!'

A dozen or more hefty black and white cows shambled across to sniff at the bed. They snuffled and mooed, so close that Gina could smell the wet grass they'd been chewing at, on their breath. By the time the bed castors were free of the grid, her rest time was up.

'Come on, Mum. Your turn to take the weight off

your feet. And look, the sun's coming out.' Her mood was changing, along with the weather. Seven miles wasn't so *very* much further, after all.

By two-thirty though, she'd changed her mind. They'd not even managed a proper stop for lunch. Instead, each person whose turn it was to rest on the bed took a pack of sandwiches out, and sipped at a hot drink from a vacuum flask. Gina had longed to take her trainers off while she was stretched out, but Bart warned her that would be a mistake.

'Your feet are bound to swell up, and you'll never be able to get them on again.'

Hardly any cars were passing in either direction. I'm not surprised, Gina thought. Everybody except us is relaxing in front of the TV, or watching football – or dancing at Tamsin's terrific party.

Roxanne noticed a signpost up ahead.

'I'm sorry, Mrs Reed,' she said, 'but Cathy and I thought we'd have reached the City General by this time. Our next shift back at St Saviour's starts soon. If we're to fit in a shower and a quick snooze before then, we ought to be thinking about getting back to Upperleigh.'

'Perhaps there'll be a phone box in the next village we come to,' Cathy suggested, 'and we'll be able to ring for a taxi?'

Mum murmured, 'Yes. Good idea.' But Gina guessed she must be wondering how the three of them who'd be left would manage to keep the bed moving? The two nurses spotted a phone box in the next lay-by and went to try their luck.

'Do you reckon we should end the Bed Push here?' Bart asked Mum. 'Tell the sponsors we made it most of the way, and they only need cough up three quarters of the money they pledged?'

'If we do that, there'll be no pictures in the *Mid Shires Weekly*. And the MP who expected to meet us at the City General will feel awfully let down.'

Gina knew that the *Weekly* was a far more important paper than their own little *Upperleigh Gazette*. Besides, the MP was hardly likely to back their fight for St Saviour's, if they went back on their promise to discuss the arguments against closure with him.

'We'd better wave goodbye to Roxanne and Cathy, hadn't we? And keep on going,' she said.

'But Gina – your feet are beginning to blister, aren't they? You haven't said a word, but I've noticed you limping,' Mum told her.

'They're not so bad,' claimed Gina. 'I can walk a bit further, at any rate,' she added, honestly. So when the two nurses came out from the phone box looking pleased, Mum called, 'Thanks for your help, you two!' And the Bed Push went on.

After another mile, Bart said, 'Mrs Reed, I don't want to discourage you, but our pace is getting slower and slower. Surely the MP you were hoping to meet must have moved on to another appointment, by this time?'

'Please, Jesus,' Gina began to pray, 'I don't want to let Mum down, but my feet are hurting –'

Quite without warning, a big old car pulled up to a noisy halt on the opposite side of the road. Bart, Mum and Gina stood staring, as the driver and three elderly passengers clambered out. The driver saluted, briskly. He was bald now, and had shaved off his huge RAF moustache, but there was no mistaking the officer who'd stood under the mulberry tree in the garden at St Saviour's, in Mrs Stott's photo.

'Mrs Reed? Gavin Murdoch, at your service,' he announced.

'Dusty Miller,'

'Ginger Todd,'

'Spud Murphy,' his passengers introduced themselves, crossing the road in single file.

'They're the airmen Graham's gran nursed, during the war,' Gina explained to Bart.

'That's us,' Spud Murphy agreed cheerfully. He was short and bandy-legged, with watery blue eyes under an untidy thatch of grey hair. 'We took Birdie Stott out to lunch, bless her, then went to visit St Saviour's. The girl at the reception desk told us we'd find you somewhere along this route.'

'Less chat and more action, Murphy!' Wing Commander Murdoch broke in. 'Ginger, you'd better drive on and meet us at the City General, so we'll have transport back to Upperleigh for the bed pushers. You, young man – do you fancy a lift with Ginger?'

'Not likely!' declared Bart. 'Now we've got reinforcements, I'm all for doing what we set out to do.'

'Good man,' the retired Wing Commander approved. 'Hop on the bed, ladies. We men will deliver you to the City General. Squadron – chocks away!'

Squashed up beside Mum on the bed, Gina didn't know whether to laugh or cry.

'I was only just starting to pray for help,' she whispered shakily. 'I hadn't even worked out what kind of help to ask for.'

'I'm sure Jesus knew, without having to be told,' Mum said. 'He saw what a terrific effort you'd been making to keep up with the rest of us, and not make a fuss about how rotten you were feeling.'

'But there must be millions and millions of people in trouble – millions and millions more prayers that he's having to listen to –'

'There always are,' Mum said simply. 'Still, because Jesus is the Son of God, and because he loves us all, we can always be sure our prayers will be heard. Of course, they may be answered in unexpected ways –'

'*Very* unexpected,' giggled Gina. She was watching the looks on the faces of startled shoppers, as Wing Commander Murdoch and his men arrived in the city suburbs, singing at the top of their voices, 'Coming in on a wing and a prayer.'

Chapter Ten

Ginger Todd was waiting for the bed pushers in the City General Hospital Car Park. When they all arrived at the hospital information desk, pushing the bed at a smart, military pace, a fair haired man in a tweed suit stepped forward to greet them.

'I'm Howard Comber, Member of Parliament for Upperleigh and District.'

'You've been waiting for us?' Mum asked. 'But that's tremendous! We must be well over an hour late.'

'More like an hour and a half,' he confirmed, smiling broadly. 'But I have to confess, Mrs Reed – there were *two* groups of protesters I'd promised to meet here today. I've just come away from my appointment with the second group.'

'The photographer from the *Mid Shires Weekly* couldn't stay on,' the woman on the information desk switchboard explained. 'He said to tell you he was sorry, but he'd been sent to cover a smash and grab raid at one of our local jewellery stores.'

Howard Comber nodded.

'That's right,' he agreed. 'And I'm not sure how to tell you this, when it's obvious you've all put in such a fantastic effort to bring that bed from St Saviour's. But I look after the interests of people in the area around Riversmeet, too.'

'Oh. There's a plan to close Riversmeet Hospital at the same time as St Saviour's, isn't there?' Gina remembered.

'Precisely. The members of the Riversmeet Committee came here today carrying a giant thermometer. They'd filled the thermometer with hundreds of coloured balls, each ball representing a dozen people who'd be in serious difficulties without a local hospital. I have to say, their arguments for special consideration were very convincing. The bus service between their part of the county and the city here packs up at five in the afternoon, for instance. Evening visits to patients would be impossible for those who don't own their own cars.'

'You're not telling me we came all this way for nothing, are you?' Mum blurted out. For a moment, Gina thought, she had the same look as Charlie, when he was yelling 'It's not fair!'

Wing Commander Murdoch shook his head reassuringly.

'Don't upset yourself, dear lady. The final decision on which hospital remains open is bound to depend on a great many different factors. I'm sure you'll agree, Mr Comber, that St Saviour's with its long tradition of care, has a good chance of surviving?'

He introduced Dusty, Spud and Ginger to the MP.

'Not one of us would have got through the War without the skills of the staff there,' he explained.

Shyly, Gina whispered her own connection with the hospital. 'I was a premature baby. They kept me alive, too.'

'Well, there's no doubt that St Saviour's must be a very special place,' said the MP, 'to command the loyalty of patients of all ages from – twelve, is it?'

'No, Gina's only eleven,' Mum put in.

'From eleven to –'

'Seventy-five!' Spud Murphy announced, with a grin.

Bart had gone to look at Riversmeet's model thermometer.

'It's a bit like counting beans in a jar,' he said, 'but

I'd estimate our St Saviour's petition has the signatures of as many people as are represented here. And we're hoping to collect still more, aren't we, Mrs Reed?'

'Once we've got our strength back,' Mum muttered. She seemed to be swaying on her feet.

'Splendid!' said the MP. 'Remember,' he encouraged them, 'a total of four hospitals is being considered for closure and two of those will undoubtedly remain open. Goodbye just now!'

Gina slept all the way home, in Wing Commander Murdoch's comfortable car. She spent the best part of Sunday in bed too, sometimes flipping lazily through a pile of her old pop magazines. One magazine had a poster of Tamsin's favourite Australian singing group. That was enough to remind her. The disco party may have been held yesterday, she thought, but Tamsin's actual birthday is tomorrow.

She pattered downstairs in dressing gown and slippers, to have a word with Charlie.

'If you're going to see Jacko this afternoon, could you pop this parcel in at Tamsin's on your way? It's the purse I bought as her birthday present.'

Charlie made a face.

'Jacko's been told to stay in his room all day. His mum got mad at him, yesterday. Still, I'm going to watch the blokes in the Model Aero Club fly their planes, up on the Common. That big posh house Tamsin lives in faces the Common, doesn't it?'

'Then you'll play postman for me? Great!' Gina tossed the parcel across to him, and took Tibby back up to her room with her. He'll make a good hot water bottle, she decided drowsily.

When she got to school next day, everyone in 2B seemed to be talking about Tamsin's party.

'The lighting effects were terrific.'

'That DJ! Wasn't he brill?'

'Reminded me of that presenter on Saturday morning TV – the one who wears those fabby baseball shirts –'

Brenda Tomlin, however, was looking queasy.

'I think the chicken vol-au-vents were *off*,' she declared. 'They tasted a bit peculiar at the time, but I didn't like to say anything. And I had the most awful stomach pains all day yesterday.'

'The cheek of it!' Tamsin muttered to Gina. 'Blaming the grub at my party for her rotten tummy ache! If you'd seen the way she was chomping through everything in sight, you wouldn't be surprised she feels groggy. Her middle name must be Dustbin.'

Then Tamsin put a hand in her pocket.

'Hey, Gina – I liked this neat purse you sent me. Handy for carrying the dinner money, right? Your card was the prettiest one I got, too.'

'Glad you liked it,' Gina said, pleased. 'I looked in all the local shops for one that had something to do with horses, because I know you're keen on them. And the baby foal has such a sweet face, doesn't he?' She was glad Tamsin wanted to forget all the nastiness, and be friends again.

There was still one niggling worry at the back of her mind, though. Would Tamsin come out with more rude remarks about people who went to church, or spent their Saturdays fighting to save the local hospital? But Tamsin seemed determined to steer clear of both subjects.

'Fancy coming round to my house for tea?' she asked. 'You haven't seen the new bike I got for my birthday yet, have you? And if you borrow my old one, we can go for a ride round.'

Tamsin's new bike turned out to be designed for mountain cycling.

'Look at all those gears! I still haven't worked out which to use on hills yet. But it goes mega-fast on the flat,' she boasted. 'Do you think I'd look good in those tight satiny shorts that racing cyclists wear? They come in all sorts of cool colours – acid green, kingfisher blue –'

Gina said, 'I heard on the radio the other day that racing cyclists shave their legs, so the hairs on them don't slow them down.'

'Well my legs aren't hairy,' Tamsin giggled, 'so there's nothing to stop me winning every race I go in for! Let's get going, shall we?'

Nodding, Gina went to fetch her friend's original bike out from the Gerards' garden shed.

'You haven't kept it in very good nick, have you?' she asked, eyeing the rusty chain doubtfully.

'I knew I was bound to get this super new one if I went on at Dad long enough. So what was the point?' Tamsin shrugged.

Gina thought, I mustn't start criticising her, just when she's being nice to me again.

'I suppose,' she said carefully, 'that Charlie and I don't get new things bought for us as often as you do. That's why we try to make them last longer.'

'Sounds potty to me. I mean, your Dad's not really poor, is he? And money's for spending, that's what my father says!'

She sped away, with Gina creaking and squeaking after her.

'See what I mean? That old bike is rubbish!'

No, it's not, Gina argued silently. It could be as good as new, if you'd take some trouble over it. But you've let it get in such a state that I'm never going to be able to catch up with you, no matter how hard I pedal.

Charlie was positively fizzing with excitement that evening.

'Dad's coming home this weekend!' he rushed down the garden path to tell her.

'Just till the Monday?' she asked, 'or is his job in

Sheffield over at last?'

'Almost,' Charlie grinned. 'There'll be a Grand Opening at the supermarket he's been training staff for, of course. He'll have to be there for that. But he told me on the phone, we're going to be seeing more of him from now on –'

'Great!'

Mum was in a bubbly mood too.

'I'd never have thought of this, if I hadn't got talking to Wing Commander Murdoch about his years in the RAF. But it's high time our fight to keep St Saviour's open took to to the air.'

'Hey!' said Charlie, 'is he going to fly over Upperleigh and write messages with the vapour trail from his plane?' He stuck his arms out like wings, and dodged around the front room shouting, 'Tango Alpha, are you receiving me? Over!' Tibby glared up at him from the rug, green eyes wide with outrage.

'Mind you don't crashland on the cat,' warned Mum.

She showed him a silver balloon.

'We're going to release dozens of these over Upperleigh. They'll all show the same slogan – WE'RE AIRING OUR VIEWS. ST SAVIOUR'S MUST STAY. I thought that up myself. But there'll be something else, something even bigger, up in the sky for people to look at.'

Not *another* of your secrets, Mum, thought Gina. This time though, Mum wanted to share it.

'Even though the Wing Commander doesn't have a pilot's licence any more, he's got involved with a hobby that still lets him take to the skies. He's a hot air balloonist. And he's going to let me be his passenger, next Saturday!'

'You're actually going up in a balloon?' Charlie sounded flabbergasted.

'What's the matter? Do you think I'm too heavy?'

'Course not, Mum. But won't it be scary?' Gina asked.

'Goodness, what an unadventurous pair you are! Haven't either of you ever wanted to float above the countryside? I'm hoping your dad will drive the van that follows the balloon from ground level, and makes the pick-up once we get back to earth again.'

Gina expected Charlie to object. Instead he asked eagerly, 'Will there be room in the van for Gina and me – and maybe Jacko, too?'

'I expect so,' Mum said. 'It's Spud Murphy's green-grocery delivery van, apparently. He usually picks the balloon up in it, but this weekend he'll be at his grand-daughter's wedding.'

'Why are you so keen on the idea, Charlie?' Gina asked. 'You're not thinking of trying to smuggle yourself inside the basket with Jacko, are you?'

'Gina!' Mum was shocked. 'There's no need to speak to your brother like that. You know how keen he is on finding out about inventions.'

Modern inventions like laser beams and brain scanners, thought Gina. There's nothing modern about ballooning, people have been doing it for hundreds of years. And he wouldn't have anything to do with Mum's other stunts.

Mum took her into the kitchen to make a start on the washing up.

'It's not like you to be so suspicious of your brother,' she complained.

'But Mum – there was that trouble when he and Jacko bunked off from school to scrawl rude words over those posters of yours –'

'That's enough! I made Charlie promise he'd never play truant again. He'll keep his promise, you know he will.' Quietly, Mum handed Gina a tea towel. 'He's got one reason for coming with us that you haven't considered. He'll be with his dad – and I daresay he wants to show Bob off to Jacko. Jacko's own father died, just before he and his mother moved to Upperleigh, you know.'

'No, I didn't know – sorry Mum, you're right. I shouldn't keep getting at Charlie. I'm sure we'll all have a great time on Saturday. I can hardly wait!'

During the week, Gina went round to tell Mrs Stott about the ballooning.

'I've heard all about it in a letter from the Wing Commander,' the old lady explained. 'I'd get it out to show you, if my silly old hands weren't playing up.'

Gina gulped at the lump that was forming in her throat. The arthritis must be getting worse, she realised. Why haven't I been including Graham's gran in my prayers? I'm sure Graham prays about her all the time. She asked if there were any jobs she could do, while she was there?

'No thanks, dear. The Home Help is very thorough. Just sit and talk to me, will you? I do so enjoy having someone to talk to.'

So Gina began the tale of the Bed Push, picking out the funny little incidents.

'When the bed got stuck in the cattle grid, and the cows came to look me over, they probably thought I was a fresh bale of straw that the farmer was bringing –'

She could hear the sound of deep, even breathing. Mrs Stott falls asleep so quickly, she thought. What if one day, she fell right out of her chair? How long would it be before anyone came to help her up?

'Please, Jesus – keep her safe,' she prayed.

Chapter Eleven

Breakfast on the day of Mum's balloon ride was a noisy affair, with everyone talking at once. Dad had arrived home the night before, bringing presents for both Gina and Charlie.

Charlie was wearing his – a bright yellow hard hat of the type the builders had worn, when they were putting up the Sheffield supermarket.

'Come in handy, this will. On days when it's raining cats and dogs,' he sniggered over his eggs and bacon. It was terrific to hear him laughing at his own awful jokes again. Having Dad back with us is the greatest present of all, Gina thought.

Dad turned to Mum. Even with both of them sitting down, he was head and shoulders taller than she was. The Long and the Short of It, that was his nickname for them.

'How about borrowing Charlie's crash helmet, in case you come down to earth with a huge bump?' he suggested.

'Bob! You don't think we will, do you?'

'Never in a million years,' he said. 'Not with that old Wing Commander you were telling me about, in charge. Think how many damaged planes he must have brought down safely during the War.'

Oh, but he did end up in Mrs Stott's ward at St Saviour's after crashing one of them, Gina remembered. She kept her thoughts to herself. Mum must have enough butterflies fluttering around in her stomach already, without a jittery daughter adding to them.

'Anyway,' Dad wanted to know, 'what's the plan of action?'

'We're meeting up on the Common,' Mum explained. 'The balloon is there already. Spud Murphy delivered it last night in his van. And Wing Commander Murdoch got permission to pitch a tent alongside the van. He's been keeping watch, in case anyone should decide to creep up after dark and damage the balloon fabric.'

'Surely no-one would do anything so daft?' Gina asked.

'I certainly hope not. Still, I don't want to find out I'm wrong when I'm actually up in the air, do I?'

Dad pushed his chair back. 'I'll get the car out, and we can all drive up to the Common together,' he said.

To Gina's surprise, Charlie shook his head.

'Count me out, Dad. I've said I'll call for Jacko.'

'That's no problem. We can drive to his house first, and collect him.'

'No, Dad –' Charlie sounded almost panicky now. 'When I said I'd call for him – what I meant was, we're planning to meet up on our way to the Common. He's got to go to the shops for his mum first, see –'

The explanation didn't make much sense to Gina, but Dad was in too good a mood to notice.

'Fair enough. We'll see you there,' was all he said.

Up on the Common, a crowd of onlookers was already beginning to gather when Mum, Dad and Gina arrived. The Wing Commander had recruited several boys to help him unfold the billowing red and silver envelope of the balloon.

'Charlie would have enjoyed giving a hand with that. You can't think why he refused to come with us, can you, Gina?' Mum asked worriedly. Not unless Jacko's mum has shut him up in his room again, and Charlie's gone to help him climb down, Gina thought. But the explanation seemed to belong in a comic strip. No-one shinned down ropes made from bedsheets in real life, did they? So she told Mum, 'No. Not really.'

Soon everyone had too much to do to notice whether Charlie and Jacko had turned up or not. Wing Commander Murdoch was showing Dad how the taps on the burner worked.

'The trick is to put hot air up into the balloon envelope by stages,' he said. 'Gradually, the envelope will fill out, and we'll be able to guide it into an upright position.'

Mum started handing round the inflated silver balloons that carried the SAVE ST SAVIOUR'S slogan.

'I want you all to let go of your balloon strings, just when you see the big balloon get airborne,' she was explaining. Gina guessed that quite a few kids would 'forget' and take their free gifts home to play with instead. Still, even if they did, their mums and dads would see the slogan, with its reminder that their local hospital was in danger.

'Time you fixed our banner to the side of the balloon basket,' Mum called to her. The banner had been made from a kingsize white sheet from their airing cupboard at home. She'd spent a whole evening using marker pens in three different colours to print on it S.O.S! SAVE OUR SUPER-HOSPITAL!

While she was tying the banner on, Mum came across to look at the wickerwork basket.

'Hardly room for two people to stand up in it, is there?' she commented shakily. 'And I was expecting the sides of the basket to come up higher, so only our heads would peep out over the top.'

'Having second thoughts, are you?' whispered Gina. She reached out to take hold of her mum's hand.

'No. No, of course not,' Mum's voice was stronger, now. Behind them were alternate whoosh sounds and silences, as the air inside the balloon envelope was heated by flames from the burner. 'Just a touch of stage fright.

I had the same feeling before every amateur dramatics show I got involved in. I was like it waiting to give my Hal Whittinghame speech in front of St Saviour's too.'

'Jesus will keep you safe,' Gina said confidently. Then she asked, 'Did I say that? Out loud?' She'd spent so long keeping her thoughts about Jesus to herself, she could hardly believe that the words had actually managed to escape from her mouth.

'You did. And I'm glad you did,' Mum told her. They hugged one another for a second or two.

Suddenly they heard Dad calling, 'Come and watch!' They turned to see the ungainly globe of red and silver fabric start to move up from the grass where it had been lying. Slowly – slowly – the top of the globe was drifting toward the scudding white clouds in the sky.

Wing Commander Murdoch marched toward the basket.

'Hop in, Mrs Reed. Your husband knows when to release our tethers. Good man, that. Wouldn't have minded having him in my squadron in the old days, I can tell you.'

'I was hoping to say goodbye to Charlie first,' Mum said as she hesitated, one hand on the basket. 'Gina, where has your brother got to?'

'I can't see him, Mum,' Gina had to admit. When I called you a pig, Charlie Reed, she thought, I was being unfair to pigs. You *knew* how important today was for Mum, you *knew*.

'I really don't think we should wait any longer, Mrs Reed,' the Wing Commander murmured. 'Conditions for the flight are ideal. Wind speed, everything –'

'All right.'

Mum was clambering over the rim of the balloon basket now. Tubby and clumsy, but so brave. The retired airman joined her and stood to attention at her side.

'Let go if you please, Mr Reed. Excellent, excellent.'

The little silver balloons began floating up on all sides, as the huge hot air balloon left the ground.

'Hooray!' the people in the crowd cheered. 'Save St Saviour's!'

Dad came to join Gina, beside the van.

'Still no sign of Charlie and his friend?'

''Fraid not, Dad.' People were already drifting across the Common, tipping their heads right back as they walked, so they could watch the balloon climb higher and higher as it glided away.

'Well, we can't hang around waiting for them to turn up. The Wing Commander wants us to keep the balloon in sight from the van the whole time, so as to be ready to help when it lands. Surely I made that clear to him over breakfast?'

'Mmmh.' Gina agreed.

'Gina? What is that "mmmh" supposed to mean? Has Charlie been playing up while I've been away? Did you half expect him and the other boy to change their mind about coming?' Dad was climbing into the van as he spoke. Gina opened the door on the passenger side and slid into the seat alongside him.

'Well?' he pressed. 'Did you, or didn't you?'

'Charlie seemed really keen on this latest stunt of Mum's,' said Gina. 'I keep thinking he must have some good reason for not turning up. It's just that I can't work out what it is.'

Dad already had the engine running, when Tamsin pelted towards them.

'I was watching the balloon go up from my bedroom window,' she said breathlessly. 'Gina, I could hardly believe that was your mum getting into the basket! Isn't she brave? Do you think I could come with you, if you're going to follow on behind to see that she lands ok?'

'Can she, Dad?' asked Gina.

'Good idea. Three pairs of eyes checking the route will be better than two,' Dad decided. And then they were away, bucketing over the stony track that led across the Common.

'The wind's changing, Mr Reed! The balloon's veering to the left a bit,' Tamsin reported.

'That's right, Dad. Look, once we've come off the Common, we can make a left turn too. There's a side road, going towards Middle Taynton.'

The chase continued.

'You didn't *mind* me pushing myself in, did you, Gina?' Tamsin asked.

'Course not.'

'Only sometimes –' Tamsin went on, sounding much less sure of herself than she usually did, 'you'd rather go off on your own – to that Monday evening Youth Club.'

At last, here was Gina's chance to set the record straight.

'It's a church youth club,' she said, 'and I didn't suggest you joining, because I thought you were against everything connected with the church. The Youth Leader who runs it, Bart Ellis, is great – terrific badminton player, keen on all sorts of sports. But he's what your father would call a God Botherer.'

'Oh,' muttered Tamsin.

'Look here, Gina,' Dad put in, 'You're not suggesting you *won't* take Tamsin along to the club one evening, are you? Not very friendly now, is it?' He steered the van in reverse to get back to the side turning they'd missed, because they were talking.

Gina was thinking, how strange. All the time I've been worrying that Tamsin was getting ready to ditch me, she's been feeling the same way about me. That must be why she's been so edgy lately.

'Come with me on Monday. See how you like the club,' she suggested. 'Bart's got plans for an orienteering trip soon, and I think he may be taking us to a Christian rock festival in his minibus. But we're all expected to attend church regularly. What would your father say?'

Back to her old style, Tamsin boasted, 'No problems there! I can twist him round my little finger!' But Gina had something else on her mind.

'Look, Dad – doesn't the balloon seem to be losing height? Will they be coming down soon?'

'You could be right. Where's the nearest big flat field?' Gina checked the map Mum had given her.

'Right over the far side of those woods –'

'There's a green lane through those woods,' Tamsin shouted. 'Turn now, Mr Reed. NOW!'

Gina grinned.

'You're going to be a wiz when it comes to orienteering,' she predicted. They came out of the trees on a long straight track with fields on either side.

'We're on what used to be Middle Taynton Airfield,' Dad said. 'The Wing Commander shouldn't have any difficulties now. He must have come back to base here a thousand times.'

They watched the balloon lose height.

'The runway was dug up years ago,' Dad went on, 'but that old brick outbuilding with the tractor parked beside it used to be one of the airmen's living quarters. And at the far edge of the field, you can just see the ruins of the old control tower.'

There was a 'BUMP!' as the wicker basket hit the ground a hundred yards ahead, and toppled sideways.

'Mum! Mum! Mum!' Gina started running across the field. 'Are you all right? What was it like? Could you see us following you?'

In an amazingly short time, the red and silver balloon envelope flattened itself and lay still. Mum was on her feet, now.

'Gina, it was gorgeous. Fantastic views! And yes, we spotted the van several times. You did a terrific job of keeping up with us, didn't they, Wing Commander?'

'First rate!' he approved.

He began to give instructions for the careful folding of the delicate balloon fabric. A farmer arrived by tractor to see what was going on. He read Gina's banner slogan out loud.

'S.O.S. SAVE OUR SUPER-HOSPITAL. You're talking about Middle Taynton Hospital, are you? Finest little unit in the county, that is. Wouldn't like to lose it, I can tell you.'

'Must have been built since the War, though,' said the Wing Commander. 'St Saviour's, at Upperleigh, that's where I was sent after I pranged my Spitfire in the woodland back there – and *that's* the hospital my friends and I are fighting to keep open, sir.'

Tamsin was getting fidgety.

'I'm starving,' she whispered to Gina. Dad overheard her, and promised, 'We'll drop you at your house in plenty of time for lunch. We've got to go back to the Common anyway, to pick up our car. Then the Wing Commander can return Spud Murphy's van to where it belongs.'

'Do you think Charlie will be waiting for us on the Common? Or at home?' Mum asked anxiously.

'One or the other, I want a word with him,' Dad declared. 'He let you down, today. That's no way for a son of mine to behave!'

Chapter Twelve

They found Charlie in the kitchen, at home. He opened his mouth to speak, but Mum wouldn't give him a chance.

'Own up now! What did you and Jacko find to do that was so much more interesting than watching me take to the skies? Playing knock down ginger, were you? Hurling stones at the windows of some derelict house?'

'No, Mum.' Charlie was staring down at the kitchen table, his voice little more than a whisper. 'I had to take Jacko to St Saviour's.'

'You had to take – why, what was the matter with him?' Mum began.

'Easy, love,' Dad said, putting a hand on her arm. 'He's had a shock, can't you see?'

'Jacko was in an accident, was he?' Gina guessed encouragingly. She was smiling at her brother, trying to let him know, it's all right. You can tell us. We're family, remember?

'How it happened was this –' Charlie blurted out, then asked, 'Does Dad know, Mum? About Jacko and me bunking off with our spray cans?'

'I heard,' Dad nodded. 'I also heard you'd promised never to do anything so stupid again.'

'Yes, well – that's the point! *I* stopped – but Jacko kept thinking up crazier and crazier places where he wanted to scrawl his name. That's why his Mum was mad at him last weekend. She'd looked down from the top deck of a bus, and seen a huge great JACKO scrawled on the roof of a bus shelter.'

'Hadn't anyone seen him climbing up onto the roof?' Gina asked.

'Course not. He waited till after dark. Anyhow, yesterday he suddenly remembered he'd left another of his signs on the warehouse at the back of Sunglow Superstore. He asked me to be his lookout man, while he was scrubbing it off – only I couldn't go last night, because I knew Dad was coming home –'

'So – this morning?' Dad prompted.

'This morning Jacko was working his way along the car park wall behind the superstore, trying to reach the warehouse – but he lost his balance and fell. Cut his hand right open, he did, on a piece of broken bottle.'

'Nasty,' said Gina.

Charlie shuddered. 'I thought he wasn't *never* going to stop bleeding! And I couldn't ask the people in the store to help, 'cos they'd have wanted to know why he was up on their wall. I made him clench his hankie tight up against his palm, but the hankie got redder and redder –'

He gulped, and went on, 'So then I thought, St Saviour's is only just around the corner! I kind of got an arm round Jacko – he'd gone all wobbly at the knees, from seeing all that blood come pumping out – anyway, we got there in the end. Only it seemed like miles, with him whining on about things turning round in circles, so's I was scared he was going to faint. And I kept wondering, what if the hospital had been shut down, and *then* he'd made a mess of his hand?'

'So you can see now, why Gina and I have been spending all our spare time fighting to keep it open?' Mum asked. I don't blame her for saying that, even if it is rubbing his nose in things rather, Gina thought.

'Charlie,' she said, 'weren't you afraid that the docs at St Saviour's wouldn't have the modern equipment to deal with Jacko's hand?'

'You don't need modern equipment to put a couple of stitches in and give a tetanus injection,' he came back at her scornfully. Then he admitted, 'but it *was* Jacko who put the idea in my head at the start. About old-fashioned hospitals being no good, I mean.'

'Why Jacko?' Mum wanted to know.

'Because before he and his mum moved to Upperleigh, his dad was terribly ill. Kept getting thinner and thinner, Jacko said. Hardly ate enough to keep a bird alive, looked like a skeleton on two legs. Anyway, Jacko was sure if he'd been seen by docs with all that space-age stuff, he'd never have died.'

Mum's eyes were bright with tears.

'Charlie, love,' she said softly, 'modern medicine has discovered how to cure all sorts of terrible diseases. But there comes a time for some people, when they've suffered so much that what they need is rest –'

Charlie went up close, to hide his face against her.

'But I was scared,' he choked out, 'in case *our* Dad had started looking the way Jacko's dad looked –'

'You thought I might be wasting away? Me?' For a moment, Dad sounded amazed. 'But of course,' he realised suddenly, 'you couldn't see how much weight I'd been putting on, noshing chips with everything in the staff canteen at Sheffield, could you?'

Mum held Charlie close.

'I'm sorry,' she said. 'If I hadn't been so busy with the petition and everything, I'd have realised you were worried sick, Charlie. Gina tried to persuade me to find out more about Jacko, and if I'd spared the time for a good long talk with his mother, this whole misunderstanding could have been cleared up weeks ago.'

'Let's not stand around raking over what should and shouldn't have been done,' Dad said. 'Is that a chicken casserole that I can smell cooking? How about laying the table you two – while your mum dishes up?'

'And what will you be doing, while we work our fingers to the bone?' Mum asked him teasingly.

'Drafting a letter of resignation,' he said. Later, over plates piled high with chicken and sweetcorn, he explained what had gone wrong on the Sheffield job.

'Normally, staff training only takes place on weekdays. But the Head of Personnel worked out a system which meant he was using my trainees seven days a week, to get the place ready for the Grand Opening. And I had to be there to supervise them.'

He paused and smiled at Gina and Charlie sitting watching him, forks poised. 'I was never really happy at the idea of spending so much time away from the three of you. And now we've talked out a tricky problem that should have been dealt with on one of the free weekends I didn't get, my mind is made up. From now on, the family comes first.'

'Hooray!' yelled Charlie.

Mum's preparations for delivering the Save St Saviour's petition continued.

'Only two weeks to go!' she told Gina one evening, after a rehearsal with the Upperleigh Silver Band. Gina had just got back from the church youth club.

'Mum,' she said awkwardly, 'Graham wants a word with you about that.'

'Graham?'

'That's right, Mrs Reed,' Graham agreed gruffly, 'I thought you ought to hear what I've found out.'

They settled themselves in the front room, with the mugs of chocolate Gina had been making. Dad and Charlie had taken their drinks out to the garage, because Dad was helping Charlie fix the gears on his bike.

'You know my gran?' Graham began.

'Mrs Stott? We've never met, but Gina's told me about her. She lives in one of the old people's bungalows near the railway station, doesn't she?'

'Has done for years,' Graham agreed. 'But lately my parents have been trying to find a place for her to move in to, where there'd be a warden on call. She loves her independence, but because they're both out at work all day, they can't check on her as often as they'd like.'

'That must be a worry for them,' Mum said, 'Still I don't quite see –'

Hurriedly, Graham went on, 'Gran's doctor has been looking into the possibilities, and yesterday we got a letter from him. Mrs Reed – he reckons the Health Authorities plan to move ordinary patients from St Saviour's, so it can concentrate on caring for frail old people like my gran –'

Gina held her breath. Mum looked stunned.

'You mean we've all of us been wasting our time? When Upperleigh people are taken ill from now on, they'll be sent to the City General?'

'No, Mum – it's not as bad as that,' Gina tried to reassure her. 'The modern unit at Middle Taynton is being extended. There'll be room for Upperleigh patients to be treated there, and it's only half as far away as the City General. Most of the St Saviour's nurses, like Cathy and Roxanne, will be transferring there too.'

'Well, I don't know what to say.' Mum put a hand up to her face and brought it down over her eyes. 'Nice of you to come round and put me in the picture, Graham. I – I think I'll be getting up to bed, now.'

They watched her blunder from the room.

'I'm ever so glad Gran's going to get a bed-sit of her own at St Saviour's. I know how much she's always loved the old place. But I feel rotten about upsetting your mum,' Graham muttered.

'Me too. Still, we did what Bart told us, didn't we? You know he reckoned she'd feel even worse if she saw the news in the *Upperleigh Gazette*, without any warning.'

'Yeah. I'd better be going now.'

Left alone, Gina knew there was just one person she could talk to, who would understand.

'Jesus,' she prayed, 'Mum and I haven't really been wasting our time, have we?' She thought for a while. 'After all, Hal Whittinghame built St Saviour's because he wanted to help the local people – and it's still going to help them, but in a different way.'

She knew that Jesus was the Saviour the old Tudor hospital had been named after. Watched over by him, Mrs Stott and people like her would no longer be at risk of spending long lonely hours in pain, after an unexpected fall or a sudden heart attack.

'Thank you, Lord Jesus,' she murmured.

For the next few days, Mum went round looking very quiet and thoughtful. Dad didn't have much to say for himself either. He was waiting for news about a new staff training job he'd applied for locally. As for Gina, she couldn't help thinking, even though it's great that Mum and Charlie aren't quarrelling any more and it's lovely to have Dad home – I *do* miss being with Mum, working with her to keep St Saviour's open.

Once in a while she'd giggle, remembering the march around the Upperleigh Rangers football ground wearing those fake leg plasters, or the wartime songs that Wing Commander Murdoch and his friends were singing as they pushed the bed into the City General grounds, or the wild bumpy ride, following Mum's balloon.

Then she'd start worrying again, because Tamsin was still managing to dodge going to church, even though she enjoyed the sessions at the youth club. Eventually, Bart put his foot down.

'Tamsin, we've welcomed you to the club as Gina's guest,' he said. 'But there's no way we can accept you as a full member, if you stay away from God's house when the rest of us are there. You may think you won't like the prayers and praise we offer to him, but you'll never know till you try.'

'I'll be there next Sunday,' Tamsin told him.

'If I absolutely hate it, though,' she explained to Gina later, 'there's a club Brenda goes to, where they don't have stupid rules about who can belong and who can't!'

She arrived in church on Whit Sunday. Flowers brightened every nook and cranny, spilling down from bowls on windowsills, reaching up tall from vases on the altar. Every pew was packed. Standing beside Tamsin, with Mum, Dad and Charlie on her other side, Gina could see plenty of familiar faces.

Bart's brought Carolyn, she thought. And Graham and his parents have brought Mrs Stott along in a wheelchair. She's looking so much brighter, now she knows she'll be moving to St Saviour's, as soon as the alterations are made.

Halfway through the service, the vicar had a surprise for them. He announced the Banns of Marriage between Carolyn and Bart.

'Isn't it romantic?' Tamsin whispered. 'Do you think they'll invite us to their wedding? I'll have to have a new dress –'

The last hymn asked the question, 'Who is on the Lord's side?' We are, thought Gina. All of us. We come to church for a reason. It's our way of showing the people who don't believe Jesus is their Saviour, that we *do* believe. Even Tamsin, if she decides to stay in the club, will have to explain to her father that she doesn't agree with all his ideas.

The rousing hymn came to an end.

'We are on the Lord's side,

Saviour, always thine,' Gina sang out eagerly.

'I suppose it has to be "thine" because "yours" wouldn't rhyme?' Tamsin muttered. 'Sounds a bit daft though. I preferred that calypso thing we sang, Kumby-ya . . . Can we go, now?'

'Sssh. We wait for the vicar to leave first, then we

follow him out and shake hands,' Gina told her.

'Ohh.'

It was a sulky-sounding 'ohh.' She hasn't made her mind up yet, Gina decided. Or if she has, she's not going to let on. They began to file out of the crowded pew.

Halfway down the churchyard path, Mum announced,

'I've just had a great idea! What we're going to need, so that people from Upperleigh can visit patients at Middle Taynton, is a regular mini-bus service! We can use volunteer drivers – but we'll need to raise funds for the 'bus itself.'

'So?' Dad queried cautiously.

'So we'll need another fund raising effort, won't we? There'll be several months at least while St Saviour's is being converted into bedsitter units, with a nursing ward and a Warden's flat – but we ought to get started soon. Um – how about me doing a sponsored parachute jump?'

'No!' Tamsin gasped.

Charlie and Gina were grinning at one another.

'Here we go again!' said Charlie.